SILKEN LOVE

"I want to finish what we started the other night." Eric took another step. Lauren matched it.

"And what was that?"

He reached for her. "To kiss you." He wanted to pull her closer, to lean into her and claim her sexy mouth.

With his chin, he nudged aside her bangs, getting used to the feel of her against him. The tip of his finger glided across her face and when she began to squirm, he lifted her chin.

"Will you scream for your bodyguard if I kiss you?"

Red sparks flashed in her eyes and she parted her lips.

"No . . . no. I won't scream."

Eric dropped his mouth to hers and claimed it. Possessively, hungrily, her supple lips glided with his. Mating their tongues, Lauren accepted his thrusts by returning the sensuous motions. His fingers tightened on her jaw and he dragged his mouth from hers. "Lauren, I want you."

She wrapped her arms around his neck and he cupped her bottom, bringing her higher in a divinely slow, tortuous motion. "I like the sound of that."

Permission granted, their mouths latched again and he groaned, desiring her, pressing her into him once more.

BOOK YOUR PLACE ON OUR WEBSITE AND MAKE THE ARABESQUE ROMANCE CONNECTION!

We've created a customized website just for our very special Arabesque readers, where you can get the inside scoop on everything that's going on with Arabesque romance novels.

When you come online, you'll have the exciting opportunity to:

- View covers of upcoming books

- Learn about our future publishing schedule (listed by publication month and author)

- Find out when your favorite authors will be visiting a city near you

- Search for and order backlist books

- Check out author bios and background information

- Send e-mail to your favorite authors

- Join us in weekly chats with authors, readers and other guests

- Get writing guidelines

- AND MUCH MORE!

Visit our website at
http://www.arabesquebooks.com

SILKEN LOVE

Carmen Green

BET Publications, LLC
www.msbet.com
www.arabesquebooks.com

PINNACLE BOOKS are published by

Kensington Publishing Corp.
850 Third Avenue
New York, NY 10022

First Printing: September, 1997
10 9 8 7 6 5 4 3 2

Printed in the United States of America

ACKNOWLEDGMENTS

Thank you Dr. Delanor Doyle for all your technical help and wonderful encouragement.

Cankeisha Thomas, thanks for your advice. It was greatly appreciated.

And thank you, Monty for everything.

Chapter One

"Shayla Michaels? Will you come this way please? The doctor can see you now."

Doctor Eric Crawford watched the young woman enter his office hesitant and apprehensive. She avoided eye contact with him and stood just inside the door as if she were still debating her presence in the spacious room.

"Hello, Shayla, please sit down. I'm Doctor Eric Crawford." Eric paused and adjusted the white doctor's coat over the blue cotton shirt before taking his seat behind his desk.

A large hat with a wide brim covered her head and shielded her eyes from him. The plaid shirt cuffed just above her wrists, hung loosely off her shoulders and opened to reveal a halter top. Baggy denim jeans hung low off her hips and black high-laced workboots covered her small feet.

Eric smiled warmly when her gaze skated over his, and was rewarded with a brief dimpled grin. Then apparently remembering why she was there, her smile disappeared and she plopped down in the chair in front of his desk.

She fidgeted nervously and her voice revealed her inner anxiety. "How long is this going to take? I have to be somewhere in an hour."

"Home?" he asked as his glance flicked over her again. Her walnut brown cheeks blushed a light scarlet. She rubbed her eye with the back of her hand, then clasped them together in her lap.

"Yeah ... no. Just somewhere," she said noncommittally and removed the large hat from her head revealing a fashionable short haircut.

Good, he thought. She wasn't as blasé about her request for birth control as she pretended to be. Eric took a moment to review her medical information form. Raising one page so he could see the other he said, "I need to ask you some questions. Your form is blank in several areas, and I need this to be as complete as possible."

Eric glanced up as he stacked the pages together to find striking gray eyes staring at him. A quicksilver rush of surprise startled him as it raced through his body. He blinked several times looking at eyes that were oddly familiar, yet unfamiliar because they belonged to this young woman. And he could swear he didn't know her.

"Your mother's name?" he asked, careful not to make her uncomfortable, yet drawn to the silvery gray orbs.

"Lauren Michaels."

"Father's?"

"Hank Michaels. Why do you need information on him? He's dead."

"I'm sorry." He searched her face for any sign of emotion. There was none.

"I don't remember much about him. He died two months after I went to live with him and my mother. My biological mother is dead, too."

She offered the information as she adjusted to a more comfortable sitting position with one leg slung over the other.

Eric couldn't stop the rush from happening again. It stole over him making him more than a little curious.

"You're adopted?"

"Yeah, since I was five."

"Where does your mother work?"

"Why?" she demanded, her eyes narrowing cautiously.

Her reaction baffled him. She had dropped her foot to the floor and sat forward in the seat. All pretense of being cool was gone and her eyes had rounded to large disks. Eric studied the swift change. His voice lowered, and he laid the pen he had been taking notes with on top of the file.

"Well, because if something happens to you, we need to be able to contact her anytime or anywhere. But everything we say is confidential, and unless there is an emergency, we won't have to contact her."

Several seconds ticked by before she sighed and began to dig through a small pouch bag he hadn't noticed before.

"Okay, she works downtown in the CNN building. Here's her card, her phone number is at the bottom. But swear to me you won't tell her anything about why I came here." Her hand shook as she extended the card to him.

"I promise." He paused, then asked, "Would she be angry?"

"Angry? More like a steamroller out of control."

"Is she violent toward you?" He kept his eye on her while inserting the card in her file.

She laughed and rested her hand against her cheek again. At that moment she looked so much like his niece.

"No, she's only spanked me twice in my whole life. Once when I was six for striking matches in the bathroom, and then when I was seven for sticking her with a hat pin while we were playing doctor."

"You did what?" he asked, surprised.

"We were playing doctor, and I was trying to give her an IV. I had one when I got stung by a bee, so I was giving her one. When I almost got her vein, which in my opinion was the whole point, she freaked. I got it good that night.''

"You're allergic to bees?''

"Yeah, and milk, dust, chocolate, grass, the list goes on and on.''

His head reeled as she listed allergies identical to his own. While she spoke, she raised her hands, using slender fingers to tick off the list. Eric stole a glance at an odd formation that lay just below her wrist.

The light mark against her brown coloring looked like a crescent moon. Beneath the moon, lay three pea-size dots that resemble stars. The entire birthmark did not take up more than the size of a quarter, but it gave him chills just seeing it.

Unbelievable, he thought, and found himself rubbing his own wrist. Sweat pools began to gather under his arms and his temperature rose, noticeable by the moisture that popped out on his forehead.

The identical birthmark that was so prominently displayed on her arm, marked his right arm, too.

Eric gripped the black Mont Blanc pen and pushed aside the thoughts raging through his head. Life was full of coincidences, he reminded himself.

Even with this reassurance, he couldn't help studying her features more closely. Her small oval face resembled his to a fault, only with feminine dips and curves. She had one dimple he'd noticed when she smiled earlier that was unfamiliar to him. *Yet, she looks so much like our family. It just couldn't be. Lots of people resemble each other,* he reminded himself, and inhaled deeply, trying to calm the quickness of his beating heart.

He knew the question that sprang into his mind reached beyond the realm of medical history. Although it had medical validity, the reason he was asking was strictly personal.

Clearing his throat, his gaze bore into hers. "Shayla, this is very important, and if you don't know, that's okay.''

Eric wiped the perspiration from his mustached upper lip and smudged the moisture on his thigh. "Do you remember your birth mother's name?"

She shifted in her seat, her eyes taking on a distant look. "LeShay," she said evenly. "Her name was LeShay Evans. Everybody called her Shay. That's where I got my name, Shayla Evan Michaels."

It all came back to him with the violence and turmoil of a fifty-foot wave at high tide. *LeShay.* His mind rocked, exploding at the memory of their parting so many years ago. LeShay's child was looking him dead in his face and he didn't know what to say. He couldn't stop the thundering in his ears. LeShay Evans had stolen his young heart, then walked away.

Eric stared at Shayla and his breath caught in his throat. He checked the black typed numbers of her birthdate on the chart and they swam in his head as he quickly calculated. Eighteen years ago, minus nine months . . .

She could be . . .

He blinked and looked up from the form, her face shaking into view.

She couldn't be . . .

Eric tried to rationalize the dates and her remarkable resemblance to himself and the fact that her biological mother had been his first love.

Still, it would have been close. Too close for comfort.

Eric swallowed, his throat void of moisture, and stared into a face so similar to his own, she could be *his daughter.*

The thought was so overwhelming, it mystified him.

"Shayla. Excuse me." He coughed, then struggled to clear his throat. "I, uh, need to ask you a few more questions."

His heart beat loud and fast as he tried to behave normally. Eric glanced out the window and saw the bright clear day and knew all of the struggling existed solely within himself.

"Doctor, are you okay?" asked the distant voice. It was

almost as if he were staring at an immovable object, because he never saw her lips move.

"Doctor?"

"Yes." He wiped moisture from his forehead. "Yes, I'm fine. I'm going to refer you to my partner, Doctor Rodney Douglas. He'll perform the exam, I can't . . . I will be unable to do it."

The words rolled over themselves as he asked, "Where were you born?"

"Atlanta."

"Here?" he asked numbly.

"This *is* Atlanta," she reminded him, snickering.

"Right."

His eyes remained riveted to hers and he didn't realize he'd leaned forward on the desk until she noticeably sat farther back in her chair.

"Do you know who your biological father is?"

"No." Came the quick response. "Can I get the pills today?"

Oh God, she was here for birth control pills! A sick feeling of powerlessness shot through him and he inched closer on the desk, forcing the wheels of the chair to grind against the plastic floor mat.

Was she sexually active already? A few choice expletives remained locked in his throat as he stared helplessly at her. He could not deny her request unless there was a medical reason, and so far there was not.

It took all his strength to answer. "Yes."

He snatched up the receiver of the phone, it fell and rattled against the desk. Eric fumbled with it before finally gaining control of the instrument.

"Juliette, I'm sending Shayla Michaels to see Rodney." Before he could tell Shayla to wait for the nurse, she had already beat a hasty retreat out the office door.

"She's on her way down. I want to see her entire workup when it comes back from the laboratory." He moved to hang up, then barked into the phone. "Juliette!" Waiting for her to respond he stood slowly, the weight of his discovery making him tired.

"Cancel all my appointments. I'm leaving."

Eric lowered the receiver into the cradle then covered his face with his hands. His heart pounded with a ferocity he only experienced when under extreme pressure to perform. At no other times did he allow things to get to him. Not after the hellish two years he'd just had.

Disjointed images of LeShay and himself flitted through his mind. Eric thrust his hands deep in his pockets and rounded the desk. The plush gray carpet muffled his dragging steps and he walked to the corner window and stared out over the parking lot.

So LeShay had a child. The young woman who just fled his office was LeShay's daughter, but it didn't make her his. Eric tried to fight the similarities and focus on their differences.

Shayla's nose was not his. Hers flattened on the slope and curved softly at the tip, while his was prominent and strong to the end. But her eyes and chin were similar. Her allergies and birthmark were his. Even her skin coloring was his. It was possible, dammit all to hell! It was possible that she was his.

The gun metal gray venetian blinds that covered the windows horizontally flattened against the window, absorbing his curses. He stalked back to his desk, grabbed her chart and the calculator and did the computations again. Then he repeated them six more times. The final denomination remained the same. Exactly nine months after he had been with LeShay she had given birth to Shayla.

But was she his? And if she were, why didn't he know about her? He searched the chart for a blood type but there was none. There were tests to disprove, or approve, any questions.

Eric grabbed his briefcase and filled it with the papers that lay strewn across his desk. He piled in medical charts, and proposals for the center. One of these days he would get caught up. Unfortunately, today wouldn't be the day. He had to know the truth.

Juliette entered the office, a broad smile widening her face.

"What is it, Juliette?" he asked sharply.

"Well, aren't you just the grinch that stole Christmas. Or are Santa's little elves the only one's who can make you smile . . . ?"

Dramatically, she flipped opened the page of the calendar she was holding and held it up for him to see.

There he was in all his glory. Bare to the waist with a Christmas stocking on his head, flanked by two of Santa's beautiful little helpers. He had forgotten that he posed for the Bachelor Doctor Christmas calendar.

Somebody had thought up the idea that if all the single doctors posed for a calendar, it would sell and raise enough money for the youth center to fund certain programs.

The picture brought back cloudy memories of how he'd spent last summer. Lots of booze, too many women, and not enough good sense.

It was very hazy remembering. Dull pain returned, too, of his wife Marie's untimely death and his brother's sudden disappearance, shouldering the blame for a plane crash he had been cleared of.

Marie's death had been painful for everyone, especially her family, but Eric was now past it. When he found her personal diary last summer, it explained in bitter detail how her love for him was gone and that she planned to end the marriage. The most difficult part to bear was how she planned to pursue the love of her dreams. And it wasn't him.

Eric grimaced. Too often he had drunkenly saluted her bravado, and in the same breath damned her, too.

When the calendar picture had been made, he was near the

end of his self-destructive behavior. He had now regained his life and had some peace.

Eric squeezed his eyes shut, remembering how he had been flattered one year ago to take the picture. Today all he could feel was disgust.

"Juliette, I don't want to see this anywhere in this office, is that clear?"

"Too late." She quietly stepped aside.

Eric reached for his jacket and walked the length of the hallway. Every nurse he passed had a copy, and others were digging through their purses for money to buy one. In the lobby, patients giggled and talked animatedly about all the men in the calendar. Halfway through the waiting room, an extremely pregnant woman waddled toward him.

"Dr. Crawford?" she tittered. "Can I have your autograph?" He glanced around the room hoping no one heard her request. Silence greeted his perusal and he hesitated. That was his big mistake.

"Right across the chest would be fine," she said, giggling nervously.

A rush of embarrassment flooded him. Every available nurse was on hand to see him blush and he knew he would feel the repercussions of their teasing for a long time.

He scribbled his name on the calendar and beat a hasty exit, escaping the other women who approached.

Outside in the medical complex parking lot, Eric spotted the delivery man taking the calendars to other offices.

Sprinting, he caught up with the man just as he opened the door to another office building.

"How many more do you have?" Eric asked, breathless from his run across the lot.

"Two hundred. I have to deliver them to this office, then the one next to this."

"How many have you sold?" He asked dreading the answer. Only fifty thousand were supposed to be printed. At ten dollars a pop, minus labor and printing, the center stood to make approximately two hundred and fifty thousand dollars.

Not a bad investment when you thought about it. The only problem was that he was in it.

"I've sold two thousand," the man answered. "Once I get rid of these, I'm going back for more. My boy is selling them downtown, so were gonna hook up tomorrow and stay down there until they're all gone. Man, the honeys are lovin' these pictures." his near toothless smile didn't make Eric feel any better.

"I'll take all those you got there," Eric winced at the amount, digging in his breast pocket for his checkbook.

"What!" the man said, shocked. "Cool, man. Wait, I don't play that. Cash, brother. I can't take no check."

"This check is good . . ."

The man stepped inside the door of the office, his hand firmly gripping the plastic strips that held the calendars together.

"Sorry, brother. You know how it is." With that, he went inside and Eric turned dejected and walked toward his car.

Then he saw Shayla. Outside in the November air, she was a striking young woman.

Watching her drive away in a Ford Escort hatchback, his thoughts fled the calendar problem and centered on her parentage. On her life.

Starting his car, Eric drove aimlessly, the idea of fatherhood shadowing him. What if it was all a coincidence? But a disturbing piercing in his chest wouldn't let him drop the matter. He had to know for sure. He had to be 100 percent certain.

Making an illegal U-turn, Eric gunned the engine of the Mercedes 500 and raced downtown Atlanta. There was only one way to find out the truth.

"I've got to talk to her mother." The black car lurched forward, the accelerator pressed almost to the floor.

Chapter Two

"Clarissa, meet me in the food court in twenty minutes. I'll be there," Lauren Michaels promised, laughing into the phone. Chronically punctual, she sat at her desk and waited for her friend to hang up. No doubt about it, Clarissa would be late. Signing off her computer, Lauren uncurled her legs from her chair and flexed her toes.

She picked up the Waterford crystal clock and checked the time again. Just enough time to order her mother's Christmas present. Dialing, she waited for Geoffrey to answer at the spa.

Her mother favored the full treatment whenever she came to visit her daughter and granddaughter in Atlanta, which lately seemed to be every three months. Lauren's lips curved. Ever since her father passed away, her mother was lonely and liked to lavish them with nice gifts. She was proud though that her mother had taken some of her suggestions on her financial portfolio. Lauren had made sure she would be wealthy until she died.

"Geoffrey, it's Lauren Michaels. I'd like to order the full

treatment for my mother." She envisioned the pampered treatment her mother received at Geoffrey's Comfort Villa and smiled. It usually involved champagne and caviar.

"Is the dar-ling coming to town soon Lau-ren?"

His accent always hyphenated her name, and she had given up years ago trying to correct him. Now everybody at the spa called her Lau-ren.

"Yes, I'm not sure when. Why don't we say the Thursday before Christmas. I'll check with her before you get booked up and call back if that day isn't good."

"Lau-ren," he huffed. "Always so thoughtful. You come in, too, dar-ling, I will have something special for you. Bring Shay-la, too. That time I will try to be nicer to your teenage terror. I mean, daughter. Bye, Lau-ren."

"Bye, Geoffrey." She hung up shaking her head. He had absolutely no sense of humor. Ever since Geoffrey caught Shayla and some other kids bombing his house with water balloons, he considered her a juvenile delinquent. Although this happened when Shayla was ten, he still hadn't completely forgiven her.

The phone buzzed the moment she replaced the receiver.

"Yes, Pam?" she answered the speaker phone. Gathering her purse, she slipped her feet into high-heeled shoes and stood on tiptoe trying to make herself taller. Lauren preened in the mirror, checking the back of her stockings for runs, until Pam's voice surprised her from the door.

"You're tall enough. Can you take a two o'clock? A man just called for an appointment, but it's so last minute. I told him you have two appointments open tomorrow, but he's very insistent it be today. Can you make it?"

Looking down at her nails critically, Lauren weighed whether they could wait until next week or if she should take on a new client. Business won out.

"Yes, tell him to come on. I'll be back from lunch by then. Lunch! I've got to go."

The heels of her leather shoes clicked rapidly and she wished her legs longer for the millionth time. Five foot four was still considered petite. Although in the three-inch heels, she was at least five foot seven, or so she hoped.

In the elevator, Lauren eyed herself in the glass on the doors, dragged a purse-sized brush through her hair, and applied a fresh coat of red lipstick to her lips.

In her business as a financial advisor, she found it difficult to be taken seriously because of her height and soft voice. She had learned through giving sound, realistic advise, she made her clients' money, and that made them happy.

The elevator opened and Lauren hurried to their table.

"The diva is late, can you believe it?" Donna Grant teased and pushed a chef salad across the table in front of her as she sat down.

"No, I can't believe it, especially since she told me to be on time," Clarissa piped in, laughing when Lauren playfully pinched her.

"I'm here now, so shut up. I was on the phone with somebody." Lauren batted dark mahogany eyelashes at them.

"Who?" they asked in unison.

"A man." Mysteriously Lauren smiled and mixed the salad greens with dressing then speared some of the leaves.

Clarissa snapped her fingers. "Geoffrey. Her mother is coming to town for Christmas, and she made an appointment at the spa. I called right after you did."

Both her best friends stared at her for a second before bursting out laughing.

"You snake, you had me believing you were going to go out with somebody. Did Shayla turn sixty-five yet? You're not going anywhere until that girl starts collecting her social security checks," Donna teased, then gave her a one arm hug on the way to the counter to get more napkins. Lauren sat back in her chair in time to laugh at Rissa's expression.

"Poor, baby. Want a man, but can't get one," Rissa added

apologetically, shaking her head. Donna handed each a napkin and sat down.

"Leave me alone you sex-crazed nymphos," Lauren retorted, accustomed to the teasing they gave her on a regular basis for not having a man. "I just have discriminating taste." She lifted her chin. "At least I didn't have to pull out all my husband's back teeth before getting up the nerve to ask him out," she threw at Donna who was a dentist.

Through gales of laughter, Donna defended herself. "Those wisdom teeth were bothering him. Really." Donna's ample bosom shook as she laughed. Her dark eyes danced merrily as she tried to adopt a look of innocence.

"And how many false burglar alarms did you call in to the police station so Malik could come over and rescue you—In your pajamas, Rissa?"

Lauren laughed as tears streamed from Donna's eyes and Rissa pursed her lips trying not to smile.

"He was a cop for goodness' sake," her voice rang authoritatively. "A girl has to do what a girl has to do."

"That's right, girl," Donna agreed with her, giving her a high five.

"If she were more like us, she might have a man," Rissa commented before stuffing her mouth full of salad. "I bet you would find something wrong with just about every guy in this place."

"Not every single one of them." Lauren glanced around the CNN center scoping out the men. She wiped her mouth on a napkin, a challenge darkening her hazel eyes. "Find one, and I'll see."

Rissa pointed right away. "What about him? Mmm," she groaned appreciatively. "He ain't no slouch." She dropped into an announcer's voice, with Donna playing the role of sidekick.

"Tall."

"Nut brown complexion."

"Neatly trimmed beard with just enough mustache to titillate any pointy tip." By then the two were cracking up. "Sexy walk, just a hint of a swagger to the slightly bowled legs. Mmm, just enough to sit," they squealed together, "straddled."

Lauren wiped her eyes, laughing so hard she thought she would lose her lunch. She gasped for air as the man walked closer, searching for a table with his baked potato in hand.

Lauren stared up at him and had to admit, he *was* gorgeous.

Donna whispered, "Cute butt and he's got long fingers. They're important, too." Lauren heated, embarrassed while Donna chewed her carrot like Bugs Bunny.

What her friends failed to mention were his perfectly shaped, evenly spaced, smoke gray eyes. Over six foot tall, the handsome stranger was broad shouldered and at ease in the custom-made suit and expensive shoes. A brief image of her head snuggled against his chest flew into her mind.

Lauren felt her tentacles of interest go up and continued to check him out behind the disguise of her veiled fingers. She definitely had to agree with Rissa. This guy was no slouch.

His eyes raked over her and one dark brow lifted with a flicker of interest, before continuing their exploration for a table. The couple at the table next to them began to gather their food wrappers and Lauren wondered with an escalating heart rate, *would he sit next to her?*

His stride was long and sure and his food landed on the table first, beating out another couple who vied for the same seats. All three ladies drew back in surprise that he was beside them.

He sat down then reached to the floor.

"Excuse me, I kicked this." He handed over her shoe, his gaze locked with hers.

His voice was resonant and impressive, and a quick sensation jumped in the pit of her stomach. "Uh, thanks you. Thank you," she corrected herself and looked away.

Hiding behind their napkins, Clarissa's light face had gone

beet red trying to keep from laughing out loud, and Donna was choking on a mouthful of carrots.

Unable to hold it any longer they burst out laughing and Lauren joined them. They giggled senselessly until Lauren had to take a sip of water. She peeked out the corner of her eye and found the stranger eyeing them with open curiosity. "Was it something I said?"

"No." Lauren suppressed the urge to flirt and glanced at her friends then back at him. "We're just being silly. Go ahead and enjoy your lunch. We won't disturb you again."

He leaned closer, his gaze moving from her ringless finger to her eyes. "You're *definitely* not disturbing me."

Rissa rolled her eyes, acting as if she were fainting, only her forehead landed in her plate and salad dressing dripped off her nose. New gales of laughter lessened the private tension between the two.

Lauren turned back to her forgotten salad and chewed the tasteless greens.

"Ask him his name," Donna said through a clenched teeth smile.

"I don't want to know it," Lauren responded in kind. She watched the muscles in his jaw work as he chewed his food. His large hands scooped another forkful of potato from the skin and he blew.

Lauren absently leaned her chin against her hand and stared at him like a schoolgirl admiring her first crush from afar. He drew the fork in between his lips and turned it over. When he slid it out, she got the weird image of that being some part of her body.

Startled, she jumped. He had lifted the carton and held it out to her. "Would you like some?"

"What?" she said, snapping her head back. "No." She returned her gaze to her plate and kept it there.

"Ladies, it's been a pleasure as usual." Donna's voice snapped her out of her embarrassed preoccupation with her lettuce. "I've got a two o'clock root canal scheduled. Are you singing at Jimmy B's Friday?" she asked Lauren.

"Yeah, just one set. You coming?" Lauren tried to ignore the fact that Donna was talking loud enough for all of downtown to hear. She was also very aware that the handsome stranger was listening.

It would be nice to have a nice looking guy like him in the audience waiting for me, she thought.

"Allen and I will be there. All right, Rissa, keep your nose clean. Bye, diva," she teased Lauren.

"I've got to go, too." Rissa rose from the table, and gathered the remainder of her salad together shoving it in a bag.

Lauren slipped her feet into her shoes and was at her side in an instant. "I'll walk with you," she said and sneaked a look back at the stranger's table. He was watching them walk away and offered her the sexiest grin she'd ever seen.

She turned and kept pace with Rissa, who at almost five foot ten, had a stride to equal her height. "Will you slow down!" Lauren complained altering her steps into a trot.

"No, I was trying to leave you." She pushed the elevator button, giving her a disapproving frown. They stepped to the back of the empty car. Lauren noticed the stranger heading their way, but the elevator filled with people and the doors closed before he reached them.

"I've seen that guy before," Rissa said and wrinkled her brows in concentration.

Lauren looked up at her. "Really, where?" Her thoughts were still on how sexy and sensual his stormy gray eyes were.

"I can't place it, but when I think of it, I'll call you. Here's my stop. Hey, are you working out tonight?"

"I don't know. Is Donna?"

"Who knows. Allen's been wanting the little wife home lately. I told her don't fall into that new wife trap and not be able to do anything for herself. You remember how that was, don't you?"

"She's just happy to be married again," Lauren offered in Donna's defense; but she remembered all too well.

"Well, call me and let me know before you go home, okay?"

"Okay." Lauren waited for the doors to close before stepping back, her floor fast approaching. Back in her office, she walked over to the window and gazed out over the Atlanta skyline remembering her husband Hank.

Overbearing and dominant. He controlled every aspect of her life by forcing her to choose between him and everybody and everything she loved including her parents and singing.

Lauren scoffed at her emotional dependence on him and blessed the day her parents forgave her transgression. She smiled and hugged herself. Single is good.

I don't want anybody changing who I am so they can be happy.

The Waterford crystal clock chimed twice and Lauren hurried to the tiny bathroom off her office. Applying touch-up makeup in deft strokes, she eyed herself one last time.

"I'm ready. Let's go close another one," she said and squared her shoulders. Confidence regained, she seated herself at the desk, and slipped her feet into shoes laying beside the chair. She buzzed the secretary.

"You can show the client in anytime."

Before her finger left the phone, the door opened and in walked the handsome gray-eyed stranger from the food court.

Chapter Three

Lauren's mouth hung open, then she closed it, staring in surprised silence. A slow heat flowed from her toes stopping at her thumping heart.

She rose and waited.

His expression was shocked, too. They stared at each other and she waited a second before rounding the desk extending her hand. "Lauren Michaels, and you are?"

His hand connected with hers and it was electrifying. She could not tell whether the moisture had come from his hand or hers, but she found it oddly amorous.

"Doctor Eric Crawford." He continued to softly pump a greeting the likes of which she had never received before into her hand.

The doctor slid his hand from hers and into his pocket without ever blinking.

Lauren felt wickedly at his mercy.

Gathering her composure, she broke away and returned to

her desk. Sitting down she buzzed her secretary, then chanced a look at him hoping her reaction would be different.

"Coffee?"

"Yes, black. No sugar, no cream."

She nodded and ordered tea with milk. They sat in silence for a moment, then Lauren said, "You called today and wanted an appointment, why?"

Eric quirked a small grin. She was good. No nonsense, establishing the boundaries immediately. Yet in her eyes lay a vulnerability she couldn't mask.

"I have very good reasons. Tell me about yourself, Ms. Michaels." She watched as he made himself comfortable in the chair.

"Very well, doctor, I usually find out the needs of my clients first, but I'll give you a little background. I've been a financial advisor for seven years. My track record is outstanding and unblemished. I teach my clients how to maximize the use of their money. It's very important for individuals single or married, to have at least six months living expenses in liquid assets. You smile, Doctor Crawford, and I know a lot of people think, that's not possible, but I'll show you how it can be done. I customize a program for your specific needs as well as provide tax planning for minors and address issues of retirement. I service my clients personally."

Eric adjusted in his seat, his body stirring. She continued, oblivious to his discomfort.

"In large investment firms, you might get handed off to an assistant who hasn't personally spoken to you and kept abreast of your needs. I can provide excellent references that will verify my work." She broke off asking, "How did you hear about me?"

He met her gaze directly.

"Your name was mentioned to me in a professional capacity." He stopped as she nodded her head. Silence hung between them and he lifted his brow to her.

"One hundred percent of my clientele comes from referrals."

Eric drew back at this. She was highly successful and smart, too. Everybody had to beat the bushes at one time or another. If she no longer had to do this, then she was worth every penny she charged. He tried to guess her age, and wondered if she would tell him. Probably. Lauren Michaels had an up front, no nonsense approach to business. She probably handled her personal life the same. Eric decided to ask the questions on his mind and see where it got him.

"How old are you Ms. Michaels?"

"Thirty-four."

"Married?"

"Widow. And you?"

"Thirty-four, and widowed two years."

"I see. Doctor, I'd like to explain something to you. Just a moment."

Lauren removed the earring from her ear, lifted the receiver and pressed the blinking button on the phone. Captivated by her grace, he catalogued every movement.

The secretary brought in the refreshments and he watched as she poured a dollop of cream into her boss's tea. The fine china was delicate and intricately designed with tiny roses. The work was exquisite, and he knew it had cost a great deal of money. Yet the expensive porcelain seemed fitting of her delicacy.

Lauren Michaels spoke in a hushed voice on the phone while gently rotating her wrist, absently stirring the cream. From her tone he could tell it was personal, then her soft giggle gave it away. For a moment he felt a pang of jealousy and stiffened in his chair.

Was it a man who made her smile?

Where did that come from? he thought strangely. There was only one reason to be here, and that was to tell her of his suspicions as to Shayla's true parentage. Eric kept the reminder in the forefront of his mind as he objectively studied her.

She looked too young to have a teenage daughter and be a widow. She was tiny! Maybe that was why she chose to walk on stilts. The shoe he lifted in the food court had a least a four-inch heel.

Her hazel eyes held a special allure that complimented her heart shaped face. She hung up the phone and reached for the earring on the desk. Eric felt his head tilting the same way hers did as she reapplied the clip to her ear. Her bang swung sideways and she righted it with a breeze of her nails against the ebony tips.

Her attitude was brisk. "I was explaining that I only work with clients in a professional capacity. I say this because your questions were more personal than I usually entertain."

"Then why did you answer?"

"Because those were harmless questions, and if you used some ingenuity, you could have gotten that information any-where. I just like to make myself clear from the outset, and only if a client starts asking questions of a personal nature."

Lauren sipped her tea and eyed him speculatively as he did her. Eric allowed her perusal in silence, giving himself time to reassess her. She was tough. Not at all the delicate woman he originally thought when he saw her in the food court. Her office bespoke her power. Decorated fashionably in deep blues, maroons, and lavenders, it would have been almost masculine had it not been for the inviting peach and rose accents.

Once he gazed around more thoroughly, his opinion changed. It was decidedly feminine. And extremely clean. There wasn't a speck of dust anywhere.

Elaborate LLADRO' statues from the Black Legacy Collec-tion and Waterford crystal graced the shelves behind her desk and the tables throughout the spacious office. The most enter-taining statues were of clowns, or ladies entertaining children. They were whimsical and fun and gave him insight to another side of her personality.

One particular piece caught his attention. It was of a lady

with an umbrella bending over at the waist talking to a little girl with a book in her hand. A little boy stood nearby with a hat on his head and stared up at the woman. The pieces seemed to tell a story and he found himself wondering if they mirrored her and Shayla's life in any way.

Her size and demeanor at lunch with her friends were deceptive. He knew he had to be very careful. She was a pint-sized dynamo.

"How long have you lived in Atlanta?"

"Almost all my life, but I'm sorry, Doctor Crawford. I just don't see how that has anything to do with how I can show you how to manage your money." Her brows furrowed as she stared at him. "What are your needs, doctor?" she emphasized.

"Ms. Michaels, I have to confess, they are less professional than they are personal."

"What do we personally have in common to discuss, Doctor Crawford?" A hard edge crept into her voice.

Eric didn't want her to be defensive but he didn't know of any way to dispel her growing discomfort.

Quizzically her eyes snapped to his hand and he looked down, too. Annoyed, he clenched his fist ceasing the irksome finger crossing habit he'd broken himself of long ago.

This woman was having a power over him he hadn't experienced before. Nerves at the surface, he felt distinct moisture beneath his shirt.

"Explain your business, Doctor, I'm very busy." Her eyes were riveted to his hands. When she looked at him again, her face was a mask, but her eyes revealed confusion and fear. He kicked himself crossing his legs again. There was no easy way to tell her.

"Well, Ms. Michaels, I had an interesting visit with Shayla recently, and after my discussion with her I'm led to believe we may be related."

"Come again? How could you be possibly be related to my

daughter? She has no other relatives besides my mother and myself.''

Her voice remained even but he could tell of her heightened emotions by the way her hand shook when she replaced her tea cup on the saucer. She rose and walked around her desk.

Eric stood, too.

''Ms. Michaels, if I weren't almost certain that this is true, I wouldn't be here.'' His deep voice was soft and soothing, but her shoulders slid up and down, as if to shake off his words.

She moved toward the door then walked away from it to the window overlooking the Atlanta skyline.

''You see,'' he continued, ''she and I share the same allergies. She's allergic to bees, milk, grass, and dust. Also, my entire family, with the exception of my father, have the same color gray eyes.'' He paused, then spoke softly to lessen the impact of his words.

''I believe she could possibly be my daughter.''

She recoiled in disbelief. Her voice was cold when she turned from the window. Her look withering.

''You think eye color is grounds for paternity?'' She crossed her arms over her chest. If that were so, three-quarters of the African-American population is related. Their eyes are all brown. Doctor, I'm sorry but I think you're barking up the wrong tree.''

''There's more.'' His low voice rang with impatience. Dammit, did she think he wanted it to be true? He didn't know yet what to make of this whole thing. He only knew he had to know the truth.

Pulling his sleeve up to his elbow, Eric extended his arm toward her so she could see. There, above the corded tendons of his wrist, lay a crescent shaped moon, and three pea-size stars.

''It's just like Shayla's.''

The clock chimed the half hour and the air in the room

evaporated. Her eyes widened and Lauren reached out with a trembling hand laying her finger over the mark.

"Where were you that you could see Shayla's birthmark?"

"In my office."

"Your office. Oh, right." She waved her hand mumbling. "Her college physical." Her voice was shaky when she spoke. "It doesn't prove anything. What do you want from us?"

Dragging his sleeve down, Eric watched with growing frustration. "Nothing," he said, then tried to clarify himself realizing how he sounded. "Not that way. I don't know."

The hum of the fax machine began and Lauren moved away from him and he sighed heavily. His sleeve hung carelessly open at the wrist and he waited for her to complete the business that interrupted their conversation.

"Can that wait? We were in the middle of something very important here."

"Doctor, the fact that you don't know what you want frightens me. My daughter is not a card in a game of black jack. She can't be discarded if she's unsuitable. I won't have you or anybody else playing games with her emotionally under any circumstances. She's had a hard life and I've stabilized it, giving her a home and love." Her voice trembled as it rose. "I will not have anyone disturbing her when she's at the happiest of her entire life."

Eric strode toward her, forcing her to look up at him as they stood inches apart. "I just want the truth. Seventeen years is a long time. But I didn't know anything about her. I just want to take the first step and have a simple test done. I'm going to do the right thing if she is my daughter." He stumbled over the word but managed to croak it out. "No matter what."

"Is that so?"

"Yes, dammit, it is. Look," he said, raking his hands over his head, his intense stare imploring her to understand. "I just want your cooperation for a short time. If it's true, then we have to work out something else. But if it's not, then I disappear."

"I see," she said, and moved from under his penetrating, anxious gaze. His frustration grew when she walked to the picture window and stared at the paper in her hand.

What business was so important that she couldn't wait until they were done to read? "Do you have to do that now?" he barked angrily. "I'm trying to do the responsible thing here." Eric crossed the room, turning her to him.

"Don't raise your voice to me. I will not be intimidated," she said, and the brown flecks in her eyes flashed angrily. She planted both hands firmly on his chest and pushed, breaking his hold of her.

"Shayla is *my* daughter and I'm going to protect her at any cost. But I don't believe I'm going to have to worry about you. Responsible? Ha!" Her voice rose to a high pitch. "Your actions speak louder than your words. Can you explain this?"

Eric took the paper she held menacingly right under his nose. He could tell what it was even before he unfolded it.

Dread slithered through him as he looked at a black and white photo of himself. That damn calendar picture was already haunting him. His paper smile mocked him and he crumpled it with one fist and threw it in the trash.

"It doesn't matter, Ms. Michaels. I'm here to stay until I know the facts."

"Doctor, your gesture is admirable, but unnecessary. We don't need your help," Lauren reclaimed her seat at her desk and massaged her arm where he'd held her.

Regret at his brusqueness made him want to take her in his arms and embrace her. It was so contradictory to how he'd felt only moments ago when he'd wanted to shake her. Make her see reason.

"I'm not just offering help. I-I want to be there for her."

"You're not sure what to do, are you, doctor?" she said, grimacing after he stumbled over his words.

"No, I'm not." Eric expelled a breath, taking his seat in front of her desk. "But that doesn't mean I'm not willing to learn. Can we at least get the test done? At least that way we can know for sure one way or another. I'll take care of everything,'' he offered, feeling as they were suddenly making headway.

She shook her head, and met his stare without flinching.

''Doctor, I have not agreed to anything. I have to think about this, and I'm going to be straight with you. I'm going to consult my attorney and see what legal rights you have to Shayla, *if* she is your daughter. I can't have a strange man walk into our lives, claim to be her father after all these years, and then walk out. I must do my job as her parent and protect her. I hope you understand.''

''I do, but I want you to understand something, too. I pose no threat to you or Shayla and if there is a possibility she could be mine, then I'm willing to see this through, now matter what the end is. Right now all I'm asking for is the test. Once paternity is established, then we can talk about everything that goes with it. I think that's fair.''

He rose from the chair and removed a card from the inside pocket of his jacket. ''Here's my card. Will you call me Monday so we can get this underway?''

''Monday? That only gives me the weekend,'' she said, but then stopped.

Eric knew he had raised a doubt in her mind, because she was at least willing to consider his request.

''Ms. Michaels, you've had twelve years. I've had none. I'm anxious to know. I'll look to hear from you Monday.''

Without another word, he silently left her office, feeling battered, as if he just lost a boxing match with the underdog opponent.

Chapter Four

Lauren huddled in the corner of her friend's couch used tissues littering the table and floor.

"I can't let him do this, Clarissa," she said, wiping the tears that refused to stop flowing from her eyes.

Somehow she had managed to complete her appointments for the day, say goodnight to her staff, and pack her briefcase with work. Even maneuvering through the congested downtown Atlanta traffic hadn't bothered her until the weight of today's meeting jolted her senses.

Then she broke down. It seemed as if every car turned into Eric Crawford, a larger-than-life figure standing over her, taking her daughter away.

Who does he think he is? Shayla is my child. I'm not going to allow some man to walk in and disrupt our lives!

Fueled by her silent battle, she asked, "Clarissa, what are my options? I don't want him to get his hands on my child." Rissa sat opposite her on a matching cream leather love seat and folded the handkerchief in her hand again. She met Lauren's gaze evenly.

"I don't know how much of a case he's got, but you have legal and binding custody. He can't just walk in and take Shayla, so stop worrying about that." In a professional voice that had won millions of dollars for her clients, Rissa patiently went on.

"But, honey, let's just look at what he's asking for, okay? He's only asking for a test to establish paternity. Lauren, I'm going to tell you straight out if he takes you to court and can prove his allegations, you're going to come out looking unfavorable. My professional advice is to have the test. But it's your decision."

Lauren felt as if she were in the eye of a powerful storm. The worst part still hadn't wreaked its devastating havoc. She rubbed her tender, tear-stained eyes and blew her nose. Sighing, she folded her hands and mulled over Rissa's recommendation. Right or wrong, the words still angered her and no matter how grateful she was to Clarissa for taking her in, nearly hysterical, hours ago, she felt her ire go up.

"No! I can't allow this. There's got to be some way to stop him," she said through an onslaught of emotion.

Rissa came and sat beside her, taking her hand. "Honey, we could tie him up in court for a while. But he would only have to seek a court order to have a paternity test. If it were granted, you would have to abide by it. The flip side, though, and very unlikely, would be for the court to throw out his request, and deny him any access to Shayla."

Lauren nodded vigorously at this but flinched when she looked into Rissa's eyes. They stared at her with a look of tolerance she knew was bad. Lauren's face crumpled again, and Rissa patted her shoulder, consoling her.

"Lauren," she began softly. "What if it's true? I thought Shayla had already contacted ALMA looking for her birth father? If she finds out that you blocked this, she may be angry with you for a long time."

"I don't care," Lauren said selfishly, "he could take her away from me. When she sees all the *things* he could offer her, she may decide to go . . . live with him instead of me." She finished in a whisper. "It's unfair. I love her."

"That's not going to happen." Rissa assured in soothing tones. "You and Shayla have the best relationship of any mother and daughter I know. I've seen lots of dysfunctional families and yours is not one of them. Shayla loves you and it doesn't matter if he comes riding in on a diamond-studded horse, it's not going to sway your daughter's love from you."

Rissa reached for a tissue, wiped Lauren's tears, and gave her a big hug. "It's going to be okay."

"What should I do?" she asked, knowing any decision would forever change her life. Just the thought of it made fresh tears stream from her eyes.

The peal of the door bell interrupted them and Rissa rose, crossing the cream-colored carpet in four long strides. Donna was in the house like a shot and at her side in the next second, crying her eyes out. She hugged Lauren while Rissa looked at them both with a cryptic expression on her face.

"Donna, why are you crying?"

"I don't know. When I got Lauren's hysterical call from her car, I just jumped out the bed, threw on some clothes and ran to my car. I was so upset that you were upset, Allen had to drive me."

When Donna took off her coat, Lauren couldn't help but laugh at her appearance. The silk pajamas top she had given her at her bridal shower was shoved into too big sweats that were obviously Allen's. On her feet were two old slippers that had been chewed almost beyond recognition by their dog, Champion. Lauren was distantly familiar with the look. It was the afterglow of good lovemaking.

"You were in the bed. You didn't need to get up on my account. I'm sorry."

"They shouldn't have been in the bed anyway. It was still daylight when you called her," Rissa retorted.

"We're newlyweds, Rissa. We still like it," Donna shot back and the three shared a brief laugh. Then Donna turned back to Lauren and wiped her tears. "What's the matter? Did something happen to Shayla? Whatever it is, we can work it out."

Lauren rose from her huddled position on the couch and hugged her friends. They had been her rock of foundation for so long she sometimes wondered what she would do without them.

"No, she's not hurt." Lauren took a deep breath and plunged into her story. "A man has come forward claiming to be her father. Not just any man. But the . . . the man we saw today in the food court. He's making the claim."

Lauren felt like kicking herself. She was actually going to call Eric Justice cute.

He's a playboy homewrecker, she reminded herself.

"No way," Donna said, pouring some water in a glass and giving it to her.

"Thanks. I'm afraid it's true. Rissa said I could tie him up in court for a while, but Shayla is almost eighteen. He could simply wait, then approach her after she's the age of consent, and he won't have to go through me."

Sipping the water, she walked over to the bay window and stared out into the night's darkness. The deep sapphire sky was cloudless and calm. It held no answers to her questions, and she silently prayed for them. Her friends joined her, each by her side as they had always been. Both knew it would be a hard decision for her to make and she needed their strength to get through.

"Donna, have you heard of the Crawford family? Rissa told

me the father is The Honorable Julian Crawford," she said, wondering how far-reaching his roots were.

"Mmm. I've heard of them. One brother, Edwin, is a dentist, and I have to say, a very nice guy. I met him at an anesthesiology seminar. I've heard he's got another brother in medicine. I can't recall the field, though."

"He has a few others that I know of," Rissa added. "Two sons are lawyers. Two are doctors and the other one, I believe, is a Ambassador. There's one more, but I don't know about him. The mother is a professional, too. She teaches at the university," Rissa offered completing the list.

Lauren felt the weight of his family descending on her head and the gnawing fear that already invaded her stomach grew. They had the means and ability to have her in court until she would be financially cripple. With a judge as a father and two brothers as lawyers, he was in the best possible position.

An intense dislike for him began to grow within her, and she walked away from the window and assumed the same position she had previously occupied on the couch. Clutching the water glass, she tried to steady her shaking hands.

"Rissa, can I get some kind of injunction against him?"

"Well, yes and no. A restraining order will be the most effective move. An injunction only follows a hearing. So far you haven't had that. A restraining order will demand preservation of the status quo until a hearing can be held to determine the propriety of any injunctive relief. But, Lauren, it's temporary. He can counterfile a petition with the courts for paternity. In which case, he will be demanding through legal channels to have the test done and you won't have any choice. It's usually done by the mother of a child to establish paternity and to make claims for child support. It's rarely done by the father, but not unheard of."

"What other options do I have?"

"You could voluntarily have Shayla take the test as I said earlier. If it's negative, you walk away and never have to see him again." She hesitated and her voice softened before she continued. "If it's positive, I'm sure you two could work out some viable visitation for both parties. But, Lauren, you have to think of Shayla and her reaction to all this. If she's not ready, don't push. If she's seems agreeable, then go with it."

Lauren sat up and placed her glass on the table.

"How soon do the results come back for those types of tests?"

"About two weeks."

"That quickly? I see," she said, as a hot searing pain sliced through her heart. If she couldn't win her way, she would at least exercise as much control as she could. "Okay then, I guess the mystery will soon be solved. How do I arrange to have this done?"

"I'll take care of it for you in the morning. Are you sure you don't want to let him arrange it?"

Lauren vigorously shook her head and lifted her chin stubbornly.

"No. I won't take anything from him now or ever. If it has to be done, I'll do it myself." Patting Donna's supportive hand, Lauren gave it one final squeeze and rose to her feet, looking down at her badly wrinkled clothes.

"My whole day has been just about how my clothes look. Really messed up."

Another wave of emotion shook her false sense of bravado but she held the tears at bay. The time for crying was over. Now she had to act.

Lauren gathered discarded tissues and threw them away in the lower level bath. In the mirror, puffy eyes stared back at her. She pressed cold water to them and felt slightly better when she returned to the living room.

"Donna, where's Allen?"

"In the car, I told him to wait out there for me."

"You mean to tell me he's been in the car the whole time we've been in here talking? Why did you do that?"

Lauren and Clarissa rushed to the window. Sure enough, Allen was in the car with the seat fully extended down taking a nap.

"Well, I didn't know what to expect and, Lauren, you know how emotional he is. He would have wanted to beat somebody up if he found out you were crying. As it is, he wants you to come and tell him you're okay."

Lauren got her coat and walked arm-in-arm, down the driveway to the car. Allen unfolded his stocky wrestler-size body from the sports car. No matter how hard Donna tried, he wouldn't trade in his first love for a sedan.

"Have you all been crying? I'm going home if this is one of those "let's-bash-men" nights. What did Malik do?" He asked Rissa.

"Hah!" she replied. "It's not me this time with man trouble. It's Lauren."

Lauren poked him in the stomach as he smothered her in a hug. His thick arms encased her petite frame and she put up a token effort to defend herself.

"Everything okay?" he asked and she poked him playfully again, ignoring the sympathetic looks from her best friends.

"Everything is going to be fine." Waving, she walked slowly to her car. "Thanks, guys. I'll call you tomorrow."

Driving home through the quiet streets, Lauren could see the blue glow from television screens and lighted dining rooms where families finished dinner.

The unfamiliar ache returned and she tried to push away the wave of fear that accompanied it. So many questions blazed through her mind.

What would he expect form them if it were true? What did he hope to accomplish at this point in Shayla's life by coming forward?

Lauren exhaled a heavy sigh and pulled into the driveway

of her split-level home. Shayla's Escort was already parked in the two-car garage and Lauren smiled, remembering how happy she had been that day four months ago when they brought it home. Shayla had practically fainted with excitement.

Now if everything Eric Crawford said was true, he'll probably lavish her with expensive things I could never give her, she thought bitterly. *I won't be able to compete.*

Walking through the front door, she paused and listened to Shayla and her friends in the den having fun.

Would he steal that, too?

A warning rang in her head and she walked in and greeted the kids.

What if this was all one big mistake? What if some freak of nature happened and they just looked alike?

All my worries would be for nothing and my prayers would be answered. But in the meantime, was there really a need to raise Shayla's hopes?

The questions lurked in the recesses of her mind all evening as she baked cookies and washed clothes.

Even in her dreams, animated men with diamond studded horses nipped at her heels, trying to steal the bundle swaddled in her arms.

Chapter Five

Eric stole a backward glance at the basketball as it whizzed by him again. Sweat glistened over his rippled chest and back and his damp shorts hung low on lean hips.

"Runt!" Julian yelled at him in frustration. "What's up?"

They were down by ten. Eric straightened his back, frustration sending his temper close to the edge. Julian stared back at him, challenging him to answer. The tallest at six foot seven, Julian had the right to call him runt. They all did. At six foot even, he was the shortest of his five brothers.

"Man, just get the rock and let's play," Eric said, bending over at the waist, sucking wind.

"Play?" his second oldest brother, Michael, said incredulously. "You ain't been playing all night. You get the rock. Playboy."

Eric advanced on Michael but was stopped by Julian who held him back. The contest of will took over as both men glared at each other.

"You talk too much and somebody needs to shut you up!" Eric said, shoving Julian away from him.

"Who, you?" Michael challenged with a laugh.

"Boys, do I need to cut a switch?"

The feminine voice of Vivian Crawford sounded from the porch where she and her husband sat sipping iced tea, watching their sons. Her voice had a conversational tone but they knew she would take a branch from one of the trees in the yard and try to beat the hell out of somebody. Vivian Crawford was the steel behind the family name and they inherited their hot tempers from her.

The yard was quiet, and even the grandchildren watched as the two men hesitated before answering her.

"No, ma'am," they tersely replied and the tension lifted in the yard.

Eric went after the ball, but Julian stopped him on the way back saying, "I'm out. Meet me at the truck."

Eric tossed the ball hard into Michael's stomach and jogged out of the yard and down the path, through the maze of cars to the back of the truck.

He caught the T-shirt and towel Julian threw at him and climbed into the bed, lifting the top of the cooler with his foot. Extracting two sodas, he threw one to Julian and flopped down on the cool metal floor popping the top on the can.

"Is it the calendar?" Julian asked after his sullen silence stretched.

Eric sighed heavily and stared out over the huge yard of his parents' home and wondered where to begin. His family had no secrets from each other and even with the rivalry between him and Michael, they were all very close.

"Not anymore. I only wish it were that simple," he said, raking his hands over dark, wet hair. Eric lifted the can and took a long drag of the sweet liquid. It felt good going down but did nothing for the ever-present gnawing that had been in his stomach since leaving Lauren Michaels office that afternoon.

"Personal or professional?"

"Personal."

"It must be a female. Anybody I know?"

"Not yet."

Julian wiped the back of his neck with the towel, a look of exasperation on his face. "Look, I'm tired of the fishing expedition. What's going on?"

Eric decided to break the news and heard his other brothers come up behind them. It might as well as be now. Gathering his strength, he inhaled deeply then blurted out, "I have a daughter."

"What the hell are you talking about?" Michael interjected harshly, vaulting himself over the side of the truck into the center, staring at Eric. Edwin and Justin climbed into the truck, gratefully taking a soda from Julian.

"I have a daughter." He repeated as collective murmurs of surprise went up ending in descriptive curses.

"By who?"

"LeShay Evans."

"Why does that name ring a bell?" Julian asked, creasing his brows in concentration. Eric felt as if he had grown horns the way his brothers stared at him.

"I met her in high school." He explained in his own defense. "She was new in town. We got together and one thing led to another. I found out only today."

"How did she find you, and why did she wait so long?" Michael seated himself by his side and scratched his sweaty face. Although they rivaled each other, whenever he needed someone on his side, Eric could always count on Michael to be first in his corner.

"She didn't. The daughter did." Eric held up his hands warding off questions by filling them in on the latest events.

"I believe Shayla Michaels is my daughter," he said. "I hope to have a conclusive test done within a relatively short period of time, which will prove what I already suspect. LeShay

Evans is dead. She was killed over twelve years ago and Shayla was adopted by Hank and Lauren Michaels. I met Lauren today and she is . . . something else.''

"What does she want? Money?" Ever the attorney, Michael always looked for the ulterior motive.

"So far, Lauren Michaels wants nothing. But if she did, I would give it to her."

"What?" Ever fearful of scandal, Ambassador Justin Crawford cursed, disgusted at his brother's open-minded attitude. "If the lady isn't asking for anything, why mess with her?"

"Look man, she may have raised *my daughter* for the last twelve years. If she asks for the moon, I'm going to give it to her! It's the least I can do. I want you all to understand. I sought her out, not the other way around."

His frustration gave way to unease. Deep down Eric knew Lauren wouldn't take one thing from him. He felt lucky to have left her office wearing clothes and not a chair plastered to the back of his head.

"When are you going to know for sure?" Julian asked.

"I'm trying to convince her to have the test done next week. She's resisting. She thinks I'm some gigolo, playboy who will be a bad influence on her daughter."

He gave Justin a dirty look at his confirming snort.

"Justin, you can kiss my . . ."

"Look," Edwin interjected, "We're on your side. Just don't go do something stupid, like make her angry or be too aggressive with her. Let her call the shots until she's comfortable. When she feels more comfortable with you, then ask her about the test."

"What does her husband have to say to all this?"

"I thought I told you. She's a widow."

Lauren couldn't take her eyes off her daughter. The little girl who'd brought sunshine into her life since the day she'd come to live with her was now a beautiful young woman. So grown up, Lauren mused, fighting back tears yet, still a little girl she watched her daughter turn her fork over again and sigh.

Lauren smoothed a lock of hair behind Shayla's ear.

"Honey, are you okay?"

"Yeah, Ma," she said, untucking the hair, patting it. "Why?"

"Well, you've been unusually quiet today. I thought we were going shopping this morning after we left the doctor's office, but you disappeared."

"Sorry, I had something to do." Hesitantly, Shayla walked into the kitchen and stacked her dishes in the sink. Looking over the backyard from the kitchen window, she sighed heavily again.

Lauren's maternal antenna went up and she recognized the sign. Shayla wanted to talk.

"What's up, darlin'?" she asked and moved to the island in the center of the kitchen. Her favorite brand of raisin bagels sat open in the plastic bag and she gathered them together and twisted.

"You know how we always talk about babies and stuff. And, uh, you always said to come to you when I thought I was ready, to, uh, do something." Shayla nervously restacked the plates and Lauren watched through narrowed eyes. "Well you know, I went to this doctor and I'm going to get some birth control pills," her head hung low as she scraped cereal from a bowl several times before chancing a look at her mother.

"What!" Forgetting the bag, unraveling in her hands, Lauren stared at Shayla. "What did you say?"

"Ma, don't start trippin', we talked about this before." Shayla turned, rolling her eyes impatiently.

Lauren clutched the bag to her chest, then lay the smashed bagels on the counter, snapping Shayla back around to face her.

"Who is it?" she demanded.

"It doesn't matter. He doesn't say too much to me yet. I don't think he knows I like him."

"Then why are you thinking about birth control if you don't even talk to this boy?"

"I talk to him, but he doesn't know I like him," Shayla repeated, as if Lauren should understand the twisted logic. "Besides, I'll be going to college in seven months. You said I should take responsibility for my body, so I am."

"I meant make your doctor's appointment for a physical, not go get birth control! There's a big difference. Shayla, losing your virginity is serious. You don't just give yourself away."

"I'm not. I'm being responsible. I'm getting birth control."

"When *I* said responsible, I meant getting yourself up in the morning and getting to school on time. I meant washing your clothes and getting home on time in the afternoon. I meant getting an after school job! Not sleeping around."

Shayla rested on hand on the counter the other on her hip and rolled her eyes. "I'm talking about one boy. Not the whole high school."

"This isn't something to play with, young lady. If you don't value yourself, who will?"

"I care about myself." Shayla raised her voice cutting her mother off. "Enough to take care of not having a baby."

"What happens if the unthinkable occurs and you get pregnant? How do you think it will be to raise a baby in college? It's not a game and it's not easy." Lauren angrily pointed out. "Your future is at stake."

Shayla snapped. "I'm not going to have a baby! That's why I'm getting the pills. Plenty of people are doing it. That's what I don't understand about you. You're always preaching one thing, then when it comes down to it, you won't let me grow up."

Shayla stormed into the den. Lauren followed, hot on her heels. Lauren tried another tactic.

"Do you think it's grown up to ask your mother for permission to kill yourself? That's what these diseases will do to you."

"Ma, it's my body. I don't want to be the only virgin graduating from high school in the whole world."

"Is that what this is all about? Peer pressure?" Lauren asked incredulously.

"I don't get to do anything," Shayla said explosively. "I can only go out one night on the weekend. I have to be in the house on a school night by nine! Nine o'clock, Ma! Ninth-graders can stay out later than me. I don't get to go to any concerts, or parties. I sit around here all the time waiting for you! It's not fair!"

Lauren stared into angry gray eyes. Once again she felt the stinging reminder of how much Shayla favored Eric Crawford. The flashing eyes and pout of her lips were all his. Overnight she had become somebody else's child. It was scary and heartbreaking.

Moments ago, she'd wanted to cuddle with Shayla, now she struggled to keep her.

"Shayla, I put the rules in place to protect you. We can talk about changing some of them, but I don't want you getting any birth control, until we fully discuss it. Calmly."

Shayla snatched up her purse, and stomped to the garage door.

"Where are you going?"

"Over to Stacy's," she said, her attitude obvious.

Lauren bit back the denial. "This isn't going to go away just because you leave the house. We need to talk about this, Shayla. But not today. Go. I'll see you later."

A mumbled "goodbye," escaped Shayla's tightly shut lips as she closed the garage door, leaving Lauren alone.

Alone in the center of the den, Lauren wondered, now what? Doubt filled her as she absently shuffled papers on the desk. She hadn't handled that too well. Her heart hammered a tom-tom beat. Shayla was to young to have sex.

Lauren blankly looked at the papers that were now out of order and sighed, exasperated. She could really use Hank's control right now.

Rubbing her aching head, she tried to keep the disturbing turns her life had taken in perspective.

Everything used to be as simple as adding columns of numbers. There was only one logical conclusion. Now, the more she tried to make sense of things, the more complicated they became. She forced Shayla from her mind, vowing to get back to it later.

Lauren opened her briefcase and tossed in some ledgers, jumping at the sound of them hitting the plastic bag folded neatly in the case. She picked up her purchase from several days ago. The bag rustled loudly in the quiet house as she extracted the calendar from its folds.

Gingerly she opened it, then snapped it shut. One glance had been enough to steal her breath away.

Slipping it under her arm, she gathered her tea cup and walked out on the front porch and down the steps. This December day contradicted the winter season, as it was almost sixty degrees. She walked around the lawn and up the back deck stairs, and marveled at the beauty of the landscape. There were still some evergreens making the serene setting comfortable and inviting. She wished she could feel the serenity it reflected.

Lowering herself on the swing, Lauren opened the calendar and looked critically at the January model. He was handsome, but he had flaws. Too thin, she thought, and flipped to February. Too flabby. March, too tall, and April too short. Each page revealed something wrong with the doctor of the month until she was convinced, December wasn't all *that*, as Shayla would say.

The page stuck briefly and Lauren concentrated harder as she peeled the ends apart. Slowly she lifted it, revealing inch-by-incredible-inch the most handsome man in the entire book.

With an extra critical eye, she stared at the picture of Doctor Eric Crawford and did not find one imperfection.

His smile was warm and sensual as if he had just been completely satisfied. To her surprise, in his ear sparkled a solitary diamond. Usually she did not find men with earrings attractive, but he was definitely the exception.

The smile that parted his full lips was accentuated by the close-shaven beard and Lauren was startled by her reaction to it.

A long forgotten feeling of desire rushed through her and she squirmed consciously aware of every second of it. It rose slowly within her, crested, lingering, making her exhale slowly.

Lauren slipped her feet from her shoes and sat on them becoming more comfortable. The distraction did not lessen the feeling, but intensified it as she stared at the muscles that rippled and rolled all the way down to the unbuckled waist of his pants. Her eyes swung across the page.

With satisfaction she grunted, finding the flaw, fanning herself with the calendar. He wasn't perfect after all. Two bimbos dressed like Santa's helpers flanked him on either side. They were definitely an unnecessary distraction, in her estimation.

"Hello," a male voice said.

Lauren jumped, holding the book protectively to her chest as she stared at the real-life version of the picture she found so hard to resist. Eric smiled down at her, then caught her wrist as she belatedly tried to hide the calendar from his view by sitting on it.

"What are you doing here?" she demanded, embarrassed at being caught.

"I came to see you. I thought we could talk," he said, and without invitation, sat beside her on the swing pushing it with his foot, rocking them. She was careful to keep her distance by leaning away from him, but held her position with her feet curled beneath her.

Just the sight and smell of him had her reeling. His cologne was purely masculine and tickled her nostrils making her want to close her eyes and dream. Yet she couldn't look away. He was admittedly, quite attractive. Denying herself the pleasure of watching him stare out over her yard would have been too much punishment for her simple crime of lust.

"Interesting reading?" he asked, and placed the calendar on her lap, his gray eyes twinkling.

"Not really," she replied curtly. "I thought we agreed to talk Monday." The calendar slipped from her lap and hit the wooden deck floor.

Lauren made no move to retrieve it although it lay open to his picture.

"You can make this difficult or not so difficult. I came by today so we could get to know one another." She wanted to look away but didn't. "I thought if we had a chance to get better acquainted you would feel more comfortable taking the next step," he paused then asked, "May I call you Lauren?" His voice was as seductive and soft as it was unsure.

She nodded her consent, and he continued. "I put myself in your position and I realized how difficult this must be for you. I thought if you got to know me, you would see I'm not at all like the man you see in that picture."

"I see. You don't have a diamond earring in your ear?" she asked, pleased when he lifted a surprised eyebrow to her.

"Yes, but it's not what you think." At her disbelieving smirk, he moved closer. "When I was in college, in order to join the fraternity, we had to have an ear pierced as part of the initiation. It's harmless. I haven't worn a earring for years and the photographer thought it would make the picture look . . . more appealing."

"Do you always do what appeals to others, doctor?"

"When it feels right," he answered and directed a level stare at her that was as powerful as a seven on the Richter scale. Lauren propped her head against her hand trying to control the swoon that washed over her and closed her eyes.

"Lauren?"

"Hmm?"

"It's Eric. I'm a man, not just a doctor."

"Oh," rushed from her and she was taken aback at the simple statement. Yet if it were that simple, why did she tingle and wonder where in the world those singing birds had come from? How was it possible that in the beginning of December, she smelled dogwoods? They only bloomed in the spring.

It was his voice.

It was commanding when he made a point but more often, was softly bass and melodious. The timbre of it rumbled around in her belly like a drum beat. It comforted her, made her feel good. Never before had a voice had such an impact on her.

Lauren stared at his ear, which was void of the shiny diamond. She followed his distinct jawbone around to his full lips. There wasn't a form of torture he could exact on her that would wrench the truth from her. But she found his earring totally, utterly sexy!

Everything about him was strong, from the timbre of his voice to the way he walked. It all screamed manliness at its best and much to her dismay, she found she liked it very much.

Chapter Six

Lauren leaned back on the swing accepting the gentle sway of it in the breeze. Eric's closeness didn't bother her anymore, but his curious assessment did. She immediately regretted her choice of clothes. The short waist, garnet chenille V-neck top, was too long in the sleeves and she had rolled it sloppily until it hung crooked above her wrists. The length of the top was good, it hit her right below the waist and she was glad she had done her sit ups this morning. The matching leggings were too long for her short legs and gathered some at the ankle, yet were comfortable. Very nice for a day at home, alone.

She resisted the urge to moisten her lips and fix her wind-blown hair. Too bad if I'm a mess, she thought with growing discomfort at his leisurely perusal. I'm at home, not in a fashion show.

"Ask me anything," he offered, unaware of her attraction to him. Completing his curious exploration, Lauren noticed the dance of merriment in his eyes and couldn't keep the wicked smile from her lips.

"Anything?"

"As long as at some time in the future, you extend to me the same courtesy." He pushed on at her hesitancy. "If Shayla is my daughter, I want to know all about her mother; I don't think that's unreasonable."

Lauren nodded in agreement, though she hated to concede anything to him. He had a point. There was so much she needed to know about him. "Why don't you tell me about your family."

"My family," he repeated. His mouth turned up in a charming grin that made lips curve up in return. *He smiles a lot,* she thought, noticing the deep laugh lines that creased the corners of his eyes, and the laugh grooves that etched around his full mouth.

"My mother is the undisputed head of our house. Her name is Vivian. My pop is named Julian, he's the quiet voice of reason. My oldest brother is also named Julian, then there's Michael, Justin, Edwin, and Nick."

His voice had grown husky when he said Nick's name and that prompted her to look into his eyes. Sadness clouded them for a moment, but he closed them in an unnaturally long blink. When they opened, it was gone. Lauren wondered if she had imagined it.

"Where do you fall in the group?"

"Last. I'm the baby of the family."

"No sisters?"

He laughed at this. "No, but I have four sisters-in-law, seven nieces, and three nephews. They have us outnumbered by more than two to one. We hardly ever get our way," he said but didn't seem bitter or angry. Just well loved.

Having grown up an only child, Lauren couldn't imagine what it was like to have so many people living under the same roof. Probably lots of fun, she thought with a tinge of envy. Lauren glanced at the calendar again.

"I have a very good reason for doing the calendar."

She cut him off, her tone lightly sarcastic. "What could

possess a man to take off his shirt and pose half nude with two scantily dressed women? What man wouldn't?"

Eric threw his head back laughing as he fielded her sarcasm as if it really were a joke. "Touché," he laughed, giving her an admiring glance. "You're right. But really my motives were sound. It was to raise money for the teen learning center that several doctors and I opened together.

"We need the money to start programs that will help teach young people how to parent. Did you know that the infant mortality rate in the United States among African-Americans is three times as high as that of any other race?"

"No, I didn't know that."

"See?" he went on, confirming his argument. "Folks don't pay attention to the statistics. Girls as young as fourteen-years-old are sent home with babies. They don't know how to change, hold, feed, or clothe. They're easily frustrated, then become abusive when they realize these infants aren't going away."

"Surely it isn't that widespread?" Mortified at the thought, Lauren tried to imagine herself with a newborn child. A warm fuzzy feeling snaked through her veins. She used to imagine herself with a baby, but that dream had faded long ago. About the time she adopted Shayla.

Eric went on, making his point. "Believe me, it's done. Some would argue, if a fourteen year old can have a baby, let her family help her raise it. But, that's not happening. The parents of these teenagers, either don't care or don't have the means to help. Most of the teens come from broken homes anyway, and the one parent they have is probably out working trying to keep their heads above water. There just isn't enough to go around, so these young girls end up with babies they have no idea how to deal with. Being just children themselves, they don't know how to ask for help and we try to offer them moral support. What we do isn't perfect, but it helps. So the calendar, while not necessarily the brightest idea, has raised the most money."

He didn't seem embarrassed as she would have imagined him to be. Instead, his matter of fact attitude made her feel small for judging him without knowing all the facts. Something she usually tried never to do. But he wasn't just anybody. He was potentially her daughter's father!

"How does your family feel about it?" she asked, letting go of the dwelling thoughts.

"My mother and father have resigned themselves that I will do anything I want to do. Actually, I believe this realization came to them when I was about eight years old, so nothing I do surprises them anymore. My brothers are cool about it, but my sisters-in-law think I should be horse whipped. I'm their new pet project." He raised his hands as if he was surrendering to them.

"What are they planning for you?"

"They think if they fix me up with one of their girlfriends and I get married, I wouldn't have such an overwhelming need for attention."

"Do you?"

"No, not in that kind of way."

Lauren sat back in the swing assessing the man who spoke with passion about helping youth.

Admiration and respect for him stole through her.

The calendar was just a means to an end. Lauren recalled all the early years of struggle with Shayla, and some of the jobs she had taken just to support them. While there were none as revealing as the calendar, they weren't all glamorous.

"I understand," she said quietly.

His eyes rounded in surprise. "You do?"

"Yes, I do. But," she hesitated, examining her own lack of community involvement, and drew her bottom lip between her teeth. *When did I stop caring?*

"I bet you're wondering when you stopped being involved. When did you stop caring about the people around you? Not just your family, but your neighbors."

Lauren felt the shiver that raced through her as he seemed to read her mind. "Are you active in Shayla's school?" he asked.

"Mmm, . . ." she acknowledged

"Doing what?"

"I help with the choir, but you don't have to let me off the hook. I know I could be more involved. You're program sounds very beneficial." She shied away from talking about herself. "Is it successful?"

"I'm proud to say it is. Maybe sometime you could come down and see what we do." Something loosened inside her chest. The wind sighed and the branches bowed to it.

"Thanks, maybe one day I will."

Lauren adjusted, stretching the cramp out of her arm and allowed the gentle swaying motion of the swing to continue. So Eric wasn't a playboy gigolo. What was he then? Her newly awakened fingers, drummed against her thigh as she pondered her next question. "So what happened between you and LeShay?"

Eric stretched his long arm across the back of the swing until his fingers almost touched her shoulder. Lauren stared at his hands. She had never been into hands before, but his seemed to beckon her closer. "Besides the obvious?" he finally answered.

When she nodded her head, he shook his sadly. "Sexual gratification. Pure and simple. I wanted it and she was giving it away."

Lauren kept her face impassive, her hands still.

The creak of the swing scratched the air with its acrid sound but she ignored it, focusing on his closed mouth instead. Eric slowly moistened his lips and Lauren was drawn by his disclosure. "I thought I loved her. I was a puppy dog at her heels; nipping my tail, running in circles to please her."

"If you loved her, what happened?"

"Oh, Lauren," he dragged out her name softly, his voice tripping over old pain. "She explained it to me one hot, steamy night. I remember that day . . ." He drifted off with the memory for a moment before he continued. "It was so hot outside, even after I took my shower once I got in from work, I was still sticky. I splashed on too much Brute cologne and my brothers ribbed me, but I didn't care. I was going to meet LeShay. We always met in the school parking lot. She never wanted me to pick her up at home. I asked a couple of times . . . My parents taught me respect, but she never would let me. I know they lived in a trailer park, so I figured she was embarrassed about it."

The swing slowed to a stop and Lauren said, "They?"

"At the time she lived with her father. Her mother was dead. I found out yesterday, he died ten years ago. Anyway, we drove to Piedmont park. I had a '75 sky blue, deuce and a quarter. White interior and white wall tires." He laughed softly to himself.

He resumed the slow rocking of the swing. "We made love and I told her I loved her. LeShay went crazy. She told me she was love-proof. She said love was only pain and meanness. 'No man will ever control me,' " he quoted her, his large hands kneading his strong thighs. "She broke up with me that night."

"Why?" Lauren struggled to find her voice, witnessing a multitude of emotions. Eric had started the story indifferent and distant. Now he sat, a solitary man, sharing with her his first heartbreak.

"She never said. She just stopped coming to the parking lot. I started seeing her with other guys and when I confronted her about three weeks later, she told me to meet her that night in the lot. I waited until daylight, but she never showed up. I never saw her again."

"Ever?" Lauren whispered, unsure why she cared.

"Never. Then Shayla walked into my office." His tone was serious. "I was so shocked at first. Numb. Scared. But mostly I felt anger. Not at Shayla, but at LeShay. She should have told me. I would have given her money."

Lauren braced herself, her temper flaming at the insinuation. "That's my daughter you're so casually talking about killing."

"I didn't say abortion. I meant to help her. With food, medicine, clothes. I made a good living at the garage."

"What's that?"

"The garage?" He chuckled. "I was an auto mechanic."

The melancholy spell he cast only moments ago was broken with an abrupt grind and clunk of the swing chain.

"I need to get some oil for that," Lauren picked up her teacup, then stood. Eric rose too, smoothing down the creases of his pants.

"It was almost instantaneous," he gathered the calendar in his hand making a hollow tunnel with it as he straightened. Lauren watched him, growing more uncomfortable, knowing within herself what he was about to say.

"What was?"

"When I laid eyes on Shayla, I saw it, but I refused to believe it. But the birthmark sealed it."

The sad expression he'd worn only moments ago had vanished. "No one can tell me Shayla Michaels isn't my daughter."

Lauren felt her heart thump hard against her chest, then plummet.

Chapter Seven

Cold tea sloshed over the side of the cup and seeped into the sleeve of her knit top. Lauren tried to control the shake of her hand as the possessive words hammered at her.

A cool wind whipped hair into her eyes and she eased it away with her fingertips, looking at him. Unfazed by his audacious insertion in her life, he didn't seem at all bothered by how much she now resented his presence.

The all-consuming fear that she was losing control, again, swept through her. Lauren stepped away from him swaying slightly. His strong hands came to her aid, steadying her, and his broad chest provided the strength she needed to remain standing. It was like a flash from the past. Hank firmly taking her hand leading her away from her dreams.

An unwavering gray stare met hers and Lauren swallowed the scream that fought to be heard from her throat.

"Are you okay? We'd better get inside."

For all his boldness, Lauren prayed he wouldn't scoop her into his arms and carry her. She resented his firm hand urging her to lean on him. *I don't need him!* She yanked her arm from his. Desperately she searched for a way to discourage him. "Don't you have work to do today, doctor?"

Lauren didn't want him in her house. She didn't want him in her life. Yet, Eric Crawford didn't strike her as the type of man easily put off, or forgotten.

"No, I'm off today." A heartbeat later he asked again, "May I come in?"

"I'm sorry, I don't think that's a good idea. I really have a lot of work to do." Lauren couldn't face him, even though she battled with a tiny measure of herself wanting to hurt him. *Don't look at him,* her inner voice warned. But it was too late.

Sad eyes stared at her with the charm of a puppy looking for a home. The curve of his Adam's apple bobbed up and down, and her resolve weakened. Damn him for looking so lonely! She backed away from her anger. "Would you like a cup of coffee?"

"I would appreciate that."

Lauren opened the door, kicked off her shoes and walked through the attached living and dining room. She stopped at the kitchen door and turned to the man who filled the ultra-feminine living room with unaccustomed masculinity. "How would you like your coffee?"

"I thought you drank tea," he said, standing before the huge ficus tree that covered most of the space in one corner of the room. The personal observation caught her by surprise and made her wonder, what else had he noticed?

"I do have coffee for company." She slid her hand to her waist enunciating her next words. "Do you want some?"

"Yes, thanks." He stroked his chin, a sexy smile creasing his face. She breathed again when his attention was diverted to the LLADRO' statues that filled the étagères and covered the tables of the living room.

He seemed to have forgotten her and Lauren quietly walked into the kitchen opening the pantry in search of ingredients.

She hummed to calm herself, and the tension eased from her shoulders as she prepared the tray, until she could feel his presence in the doorway.

Lauren lifted the tray and he stepped forward unburdening her of its weight. "Go ahead, I've got it."

It was easy to watch his large hands tend to her tea and serve himself. He was quite good at it. Drawn to the corded muscles of his arms, Lauren dragged her gaze from them to the plate he had filled with warm sweet rolls.

Each of his attentive movements chipped away at her cautious spirit until Lauren felt herself wanting to reciprocate his easy generosity. The house was very quiet with muted noise from passing cars providing the only backdrop of sound.

Lauren relieved her initial reaction from the first time she saw him in the food court. She shifted, uncomfortable with the intensity of the flirtatious feelings. She bit into a roll hoping again he didn't sense her attraction to him. Too many emotions, she told herself and not enough time.

"When did you make these? They're very good." He bit into one of the warm, flaky rolls.

"Yesterday." Lauren brushed her hair behind her ear. It fell out again. Nothing was working out right. "I microwaved them."

"I'm very familiar with that convenience," he said easily. "I use it all the time." His gaze shifted as he looked around the room.

Lauren hated to ask but had to. "What makes you think being a father to Shayla is going to be easy? After all, you are a bachelor."

Eric shook his head growing serious. "I don't think it's going to be easy. Frankly, I'm terrified of what her reaction will be. But regardless of what it is, I'm going to try to have a relationship with her. I hope in time she'll accept me."

Lauren waited a moment. "What about your love life? Won't this put a cramp in your style?"

He chuckled. "I don't have a style. I don't have a love life right now either. Maybe one day soon I'll get lucky."

His sensual charm wasn't lost on her, but she ignored the effect the news had, taking her time licking the sugary frosting from her lips.

"I find that very hard to believe."

"That it's nonexistent, or that I'll get lucky?" He winked at her, reaching out and wiping frosting form her bottom lip.

Lauren took the napkin from his hand and continued what he started, her lip trembling. "I know you're not hurting for attention. There's got to be somebody in the wings, doctor."

"I'm not going to pretend to be a choir boy." He leaned forward folding his arms, their knees touching beneath the table. "But after last year, I decided that I would cool it on the casual relationships. They don't ease the pain of losing a loved one, a wife. That only happens with time. I've worked through that, but casual relationships only cover up the hurt with temporary gratification. When that's over, the other person gets hurt, and what you were running from is still there."

Everything he said slammed into her with the force of a mack truck. His words of wisdom delved into parts she kept strictly off limits. Unlike him, she didn't want to forget the pain. Forgetting meant she could allow any controlling, prevailing force to come in and rule her life. Although she had loved Hank, she hadn't loved herself enough to stand up to his dominance.

Lauren eased her legs away, from his and closed off her personal soul searching.

So far, Eric had laid his life open, yet, if he didn't have a love now, had he since his wife died? Lauren rationalized her next question, that for Shayla's benefit, she should know.

"Were you and your wife very much in love when she died?" It wasn't the distress that crossed his face that had her regretting her curiosity, but the creeping sadness that once again claimed his features.

He hesitated, and Lauren opened her mouth to apologize.

"I believe we loved each other until my dedication to my work became more than just a satisfying occupation. I found any reason to be away from home. There was always a baby to be delivered, a father who needed emotional support through a crisis delivery, or a single mother who had no one else to turn to." He gave a bitter bark of laughter and shook his head. "I didn't realize until after she died, that I'd held more hands of laboring women than I did Marie's. I wasn't there to hold my wife's hand when she needed me."

His admission stunned her and Lauren sat back drawing her hand to her side. She had reached out to comfort a man who had said he was over the pain of losing his wife, but appeared to still grieve for her. Why else would he be filled with a visceral sadness she could almost touch?

Eric raised his cup to his lips taking a swallow of the black coffee before he changed the subject.

"Why haven't you ever remarried?"

Black holes of a double barrel shot gun might as well have been pointed at her. Loaded with innuendo, it was her turn to feel uneasy. "I haven't wanted to."

"Come on Lauren, be honest," he coaxed. "Why couldn't a man get you down the aisle? Too many fellas to choose from?"

"No."

"Gay?"

"No."

"Just haven't met mister right?"

"No," she said, tiring of the third degree. "I thought about it years ago, but I changed my mind," a wave of her hand indicated her impatience with the questions and she rose tossing the cloth napkin on the chair. "I had Shayla to think about."

He nodded. "Good."

Lauren slipped into the trap before she could catch herself. "What's so good about that? I didn't want to be alone! I mean,

I do want to be alone. I mean, that I'm happy doing what I want, when I want, without anyone telling me different.''

"He must have been one controlling son-of-a—bitch," he observed quietly.

Lauren closed her mouth and from the look in his eyes, knew he had gotten the answer he wanted. She sat down. "My husband was a loving man." Defensively she went on. "He took care of me very well and had he not been cut down in the prime of his life, I'm sure we would still be together."

"So you're saving all your love for a dead man?"

"Of course not! I've resolved myself to knowing I probably won't get married again. And that's perfectly all right with me." Lauren enunciated the last words, growing more perturbed when he smiled.

"Okay." He threw up his hands. Before she could retort, their attention was drawn to the window where a cardinal fluttered landing on the screen. It stared inside, then was joined by its mate laden with a night crawler for breakfast.

Lauren and Eric watched, riveted to the private exchange. The first bird chirped and they exchanged the worm, then both flew away.

"There's more to being in love than what the eye can see."

Lauren swung her eyes to his, startled at what he might be able to see.

Blood rushed through her, her heart escalating its rhythmic beats double time. Eric didn't move a muscle, but his eyes bore into her seeming to examine her soul. Lauren wiped her damp palms on her pants and rose distancing herself from the close scrutiny.

He rose, too. She could feel him moving around behind her and she thought he was approaching. But when she turned around she was surprised at what had caught his attention. He had found the photo album of Shayla from elementary to middle school.

"Do you mind?" he asked, flipping through the pages. A

retort was on the tip of her tongue until she spotted the birthmark on his arm again. Just the moon shape showed, but it was enough to kill the negative response.

"No, go ahead." She cleared the table and made herself busy in the kitchen away from him. Lauren wanted to believe his laughter brought her back to his side, but it was more than that. Like a gravitational magnet, she felt right there.

His hand snaked out and took hers, making her lean over the book looking at the picture he pointed to.

"Who's that?"

"That's my mother and father"—she pointed—"and that's Shayla. She was six."

"Who's this?"

"That's me."

"You look sad," he observed and studied the picture closely. Their heads were only inches apart and Lauren grabbed the jade stone of her necklace after it landed on the book and leaned away from him.

"I can't recall how I was feeling."

Lauren wondered what his reaction would be if she told him that her husband had just died and the stress of single parenthood with a child who had come from an emotionally abused background had been nearly more than she could bear?

Except for this new whirlwind that threatened to capsize her life, that period was the most difficult and tumultuous. Lauren tried to extract her hand from his, but he held tight looking up from the photo album straight into her eyes. He pulled her closer.

"How can I get you to trust me?" he asked, thrusting through her cool reserve. No man had pushed to know her mind. No man had ever cared before. Lauren felt the swell of yearning and knew she was in deep, troubled water.

"Disappear," she whispered back, her eyes stinging.

"I can't do that." He released her hand and stepped back. Lauren moved to the window where the cardinals had been, and stared out, fingering the tiny jade stone that lay at the bottom of the long gold chain around her neck. She twisted and turned it and said, "Doctor Crawford?"

She hadn't expected him to come to her side, and when he touched her arm, she turned to face him. Lauren fingered the stone again, before allowing the jade to fall back into its familiar home between her breasts.

She couldn't tell if he felt it, too, but her attraction to him was so strong, she knew if he stayed longer, more than just talking would go on. He was there for her daughter, not her.

"Lauren, what else can I do to convince you of my sincerity? I'll never do anything to hurt her . . ."

"I know," she said. A blind trust in him was building. "We had the blood test done this morning. I lied to her and told her more tests were needed to complete her college medical form. If Shayla is your . . ." her voice quivered slightly, "daughter, then we'll know two weeks from Wednesday."

His happiness was her pain. Lauren stepped back. She couldn't share his joy. Surprised when he gathered her in his arms in a tight embrace, she didn't immediately push away.

"All I seem to do is thank you," his voice grew husky. "I'm going to prove to you I can be a good father to Shayla." His voice lowered when he said, "I promise." His lips brushed her hair and seemed to slide with accuracy toward her mouth. She hurriedly stepped out of his embrace.

"You can't know how much this means to me."

It had been a mistake. He wasn't really going to kiss her. Was he? His gaze held hers. His eyes didn't reflect desire, only gratitude. Lauren wondered again why she felt this abnormal attraction for a man who was turning her life upside down. Her voice was full of sadness when she responded. "I felt the same way twelve years ago."

He held her close to him stroking her hair, then burst out with an excited laugh, releasing her with an abrupt jerk. "I'll go to the same doctor and have the test so there won't be any discrepancies. What's the doctor's name?" A crisp beep cut into the heavy air and Lauren dragged her eyes from his happy face to the rectangular box at his side.

Fingering the beeper, Eric looked at the numbers then checked his watch.

Relieved at the distraction, Lauren willed her heart rate to slow down from its marathon pace and massaged her numb cheek that had rested comfortably on his chest. Too comfortably. Stepping even farther away, she answered, "Doctor Elizabeth Heffron."

"Liz? Great, she's a colleague. I can probably get the results back sooner. I wish you had let me arrange this. I would have paid for everything."

"Just a minute!" The world was suddenly moving too fast. "I don't want your money or your favors. I wouldn't take your money if you gave it to me."

He shrugged and stared at the fingernail she pointed at him. "Fine. I simply offered."

"I don't want anything from you. Remember that! We've been doing fine all these years."

"Lauren." His voice held a edge of warning, his eyes a humorless glare. "I'm going to help Shayla in every way possible. This has been seventeen years in coming and whether you like it or not, we're going to be related."

"Goodbye, Doctor Crawford." Cold dread poured over her in waves. She hadn't anticipated losing control of her emotions in front of him. Lauren fought the strong urge to throw herself at his feet and beg him to leave her life forever. Sanity kept her rooted in place. Eric Crawford would not oblige her. He had found a new reason to live.

"You'll hear from us within two weeks."

"You can count on it," he promised, and she didn't miss the steely determination in his voice.

He walked through the living room, stopping at the door.

The sound of a barking chow flowed weakly into the room splitting the quiet.

Lauren watched his silent debate, anxious for him to leave before she lost control of the flood of emotions held at bay by a weak will.

"I want to be there when you tell her."

"No." *Leave,* she pleaded silently.

"Why not?"

"B-because, it's already going to be a shock, and I want her to be able to experience all her emotions without an audience." Lauren held her hands together in what she pretended was calm assurance. She hoped they did not reveal the pain that tore through her.

Eric massaged the bridge of his nose. "Okay, but I want to see her right after. If she wants to see me." He looked at her and asked, "Will you call me?"

Lauren managed a shake of her head which she knew he couldn't interpret. The dam had crested, and was seeping over. She tried to swallow the ball that lodged in her throat and the tears that stung the back of her eyes, now brimmed her lids ready to fall.

"Never mind, I'll call you," his gaze lingered a second longer then without a backward glance, he headed down the driveway with a determined lift to his step and Lauren hoped he wouldn't trip and fall, and delay his departure.

The slam of the dead bolt lock in the chamber of the front door gave permission to the tears, and they flowed unchecked, as she watched him back down the driveway through blurry eyes. When he was out of sight, Lauren breathed again, and walked into the kitchen swiping at the tears that ran down her cheeks.

Snatching the napkin from beneath the tray, she tried to catch the precariously perched plate that slid to the corner of the island.

"Oh, no," she gasped, unable to stop its downward slide.

The crash and splintering of the glass startled her, but it released a well of built up tension from her chest. Surprisingly, it sounded wonderful. The shrill splintering cleansed away the deeply male bass of Eric Crawford's voice and when she intentionally dropped another, it sounded better.

Lauren heaved a fueling breath and raised her hand high holding the cup he had held only moments ago. She let it go. "Yes!" she shouted, celebrating the explosion laughing for the first time in days. Oh well, she thought, emancipated. Might as well make it a set.

Holding her cup, Lauren opened her fingers and watched it flip and rock, dancing to gravity's pull until it ran out of space and smashed into the floor. She heaved a sigh of relief.

Only when everything stayed quiet for a few moments, did she walk to the closet and pull out the broom and dustpan.

Lauren smiled and "sighed." She felt much better.

Chapter Eight

"Take a deep breath, Stephanie, and bear down."

The terrified eyes of the fifteen-year-old soon-to-be mother closed tightly as she screamed through gritted teeth and did as he instructed.

The top of the baby's head surged through. "Push," Eric commanded, positioning his fingers on either side of the newborn's head. He put his hand on top of her stomach pushed down, demanding as he did, "Push! One last time."

A groan tore from the mother as she birthed her child and he guided the baby out, untangling it as he held it firmly in his gloved hands.

"Steph, we got a girl." Eric smiled at the young woman who had just become a mother. She leaned up, assisted by the nurses who aided tremendously in this young girl's journey into motherhood. No family had shown up.

Eric cut the cord and handed the baby to the nurse who laid it in Stephanie's waiting arms. He stopped captured by the sight of the two children together then refocused on the remaining tasks. The afterbirth surged forth as Rodney, his partner, entered the operating room dressed for work. Eric continued to suture.

"Congratulations, Big-Daddy." Rodney said and grinned at the term they used for each other each time one delivered another baby. "What does this make? Your forty-eighth?"

"Fiftieth. I had one this morning, too. My wall isn't big enough for my kids."

"Where are they taking my baby?" Stephanie asked, fear lacing her voice.

Eric kept her paralyzed legs from slipping off the table. Still heavy from the epidural, he knew she would have control of them again. Soon. He glanced at her briefly, but continued to work. "Remember the class on testing?" He spoke loudly but firmly. "The baby is having her Apgar tests done."

Stephanie's eyes drifted closed for a second and she blinked groggily. Her eyes closed and she fell asleep.

"I felt that way, too, in med school when I got to that part." Rodney joked keeping his voice low.

They looked at each other and grinned. A lot of women fell asleep right after childbirth. Mainly because they hadn't slept in several days. And as soon as they realized their baby was okay, their bodies shut off.

"Angel," she whispered.

Eric finished up and watched as the nurse piled monitors, blankets, and pads on the end of the teenagers bed. She pushed her away from them.

Eric headed for the sink. "We got ourselves an Angel, Rod," he said roughly, his heart swelling as it always did after watching the miracle yet again.

"That's good news." He watched while Eric scrubbed. "I've got bad news though. I know you thought you were done, but we've got two on the way in."

Eric dropped his head, closing his eyes. He knew how Stephanie felt. Fatigue was closing in on him fast. He had been at the hospital ever since leaving Lauren's house yesterday afternoon. His eyes refused to obey the command his brain sent to open.

"Rod, I can't. It's been almost thirty-two hours since I laid my head on a pillow. I don't count the couch in the lounge as sleeping. Mac woke me up when he sat on me." Eric swiped down a towel and wiped his dripping arms.

"I know," Rod said sympathetically. "Plus the personal changes in your life have got to be keeping you up. I know you haven't gotten much sleep. That's why I'm here to relieve you."

Eric's eyes snapped open. "I thought you were seeing Nina this weekend?"

Rodney shrugged and half smiled. "I thought so, too. But she's got to finish her master's thesis. She chose books over spending the weekend with me in bed." He shrugged again. "Her loss."

Eric slapped a hand on his partner's shoulder offering silent support. "You better believe she's going to come begging for it someday." They both laughed. "Are you sure, man?" Eric prayed his friend and partner wouldn't let him down.

"Naw, man, go home. I'd rather be here than by myself at the house. We'll switch one weekend when I need it."

Eric slapped him on the back and waved as he walked away. "Thanks. I'll owe you."

"Hey?" Rodney called. Eric backpedaled, still heading down the hall. Rod flipped open his jacket and poked out his gut. "Great picture."

Eric turned, waved, and kept walking. He couldn't respond. He was looking forward too much to going to bed.

Eric slammed around his kitchen, starving after eight straight hours of sleep. He fried a egg sandwich and chewed it methodically. Lauren had been crying the last time he saw her. The sound of breaking glass filled his memory and he flinched. He had gone back to her door, preparing to demand that he be there when she told Shayla, yet he couldn't see her. But the shattering took him to the back of the house, on the deck, and when he looked through the sliding glass door, he could see everything clearly.

The ever poised Lauren Michaels, who wore control like a shield of honor, was in her kitchen smashing dishes!

That's one way to deal with it, he thought, wiping at the crumbs that lay on the living room table. Watching her lose control was one thing, but knowing he'd made her cry was quite another. Eric felt worse as the eggs settled in the bottom of his stomach like lead balls. *She doesn't deserve this.*

Other more important thoughts ran through his mind. *What am I going to do with a daughter?* Confused and more than a little insecure, Eric slid into the corner of the sofa and continued to do what he had done since he had gotten home last night. He couldn't even stop thinking in his sleep.

A daughter. A teenage daughter. A teenage daughter who doesn't need a father. Or does she? Has she ever wondered where I was? How often has she cried for me to come for her? What if . . . she doesn't want me? What if my presence in her life makes it hell?

In defense of the negative thoughts, Eric squared his shoulders. *I'm not that bad, am I?*

He looked at himself from Lauren's point of view and cringed at what he saw. Bachelor, loner, widower, irresponsible, negligent. . . . He stopped, the list growing with each passing second.

What can I offer this girl? Lauren's words were like the old metal rake he used to gather the leaves off his parent's lawn when it hit the cement path. Hard and sharp enough to make him grit his teeth from the scraping sound. *I don't want anything from you. Disappear.*

Lauren's golden eyes pleaded more than her mouth and he

had indeed, for only a moment, wanted to bid her wishes. Quickly that thought evaporated like a flame without oxygen.

Despite the surprise, the missed years of Shayla's youth didn't matter. He wanted her because she was his.

The thundering anticipation of positive news surrounded him again, making his breathing come faster.

With a startled grunt he jumped to his feet. Having a daughter changed things. He looked sharply around the room. The entire lower level of the house was a testosterone-injected male domain. Deep green carpet covered the floor, while black leather furniture stood at masculine attention before the large-screen television. Stereo speakers hung from the walls for maximum surround sound, and in one corner lay sports equipment of every kind. The tables were shiny and black, covered with stains from bottles and cold sweating cans. Strewn about were various male magazines, with pictorials that had nothing to do with medical science.

Eric focused on the round metal cake pan that lay on the living room table. Dishes! He rushed to the kitchen, opening each cabinet and found none. Because there were none! He hurled a string of expletives, then dragged his hands over his face and head as he stalked out of the confines of the kitchen, through the sunken living room. He turned, as something dawned on him. It didn't much matter about plates, since he didn't have a dinette.

In the space designed for a cherrywood table, six chairs, a matching china cabinet and credenza, stood a black, leather, fully-stocked bar. Irresponsible clanged in his head.

Eric shook his head. *How can I have a daughter and no dinette?* He mentally held up his score card against Lauren's and didn't like what he saw. Determined, he picked up the phone and dialed. *I can do this parent thing.*

"Hello," the sweet voice answered.

"April, Eric. Come over. I need your help."

* * *

Standing on the front porch, Eric waited anxiously for his sister-in-law to finish her assessment. April Crawford came outside and linked her arm with his. "It's bad, baby."

Eric felt hope vanish into dollar signs, which floated like birdies around his head.

"First of all, that spare bedroom needs a complete makeover," she continued over his loud groan. "I'm sorry but it's horrible. Gym clothes, dirty laundry, weights everywhere. *Green walls.*" She rolled her eyes to the sky. "Eric, you're a pig with bad taste." The look she gave him confirmed her statement.

"I opened the window, and I'm going to have someone come over tomorrow and clean it before I go in there again. The downstairs isn't too bad. Are you sure you want to keep the carpet? It's so dark."

"It stays."

"Okay, but don't call me next year wanting to change because you can't stand it. Now your room, Eric Crawford," she admonished. "If you weren't Michael's baby brother I would be charging you a king's ransom for the work I have to do in there. Gray walls? Honey, please," she said laughing. "Oh, it's going to take six to eight weeks for the furniture to be delivered."

"April, I can't wait that long! Find me something else. Maybe something less expensive." He added at her chagrined look. "Come on, April. Hook a brother up."

"Hook—?" she started, then stopped.

April and Michael were more than family to him. They supported him through the tough years after Marie's death. Eric mourned with them earlier that year when in vitro fertilization hadn't worked for them. But they remained close to each other, hoping one day for a miracle.

Planting her free hand on her hip, April got the head motion going and Eric knew he was in trouble.

"We just went through this last year. Remember? You were in a dark, brooding mood and wanted gray walls and black carpet. We compromised and went with green carpet and black furniture. Next you're going to want yellow carpet and orange walls. I hooked you then. Not now, buddy. I-got-to-make-a-living." Dropping the attitude, she said matter-of-factly, "Who is she?"

"You'll know soon enough." Eric clamped his mouth shut. Telling April anything was just short of releasing it to a tabloid newspaper. Before she got home, she would be burning the cellular circuits telling everybody.

"Where's my credit card, April?" Eric asked and knew the answer before she even opened her mouth.

"Chil', you ain't getting that little green and white plastic cash back. I got too much work to do. Kiss it goodbye." She laughed again, then moved in for a hug. Eric hugged her. He felt sick when he sneaked a look at the total she had written on her pad.

They separated when her assistant stepped on the porch, giving him an inviting smile. She had long attractive legs that went on for days and any other time he would have pursued the unspoken invitation. But not now.

The type of legs that mounted him in his dreams last night were short, shapely, and belonged to a golden eyes tigress named Lauren.

Chapter Nine

How long could it take to examine one vial of blood? *These people are scientists for God's sake,* Lauren huffed tiredly for what she felt sure was the hundredth time.

Frustrated, she flopped on the couch and stared blankly out the window of her office as she flexed her toes, getting comfortable. Elusive slumber threatened to claim her, and she welcomed it after fourteen restless, nights. Every time she saw him, she made herself wake up. Lauren fought her dreams, afraid of what dreaming of Eric Crawford would do to her.

Two weeks and he hadn't even called. But why would he? Torture purposes, of course, she surmised.

The low buzz of the phone beckoned a response and Lauren dragged her tired body back to her desk, apprehension causing her hand to jerk before she depressed the speaker phone button.

"Lauren here."

"Lauren, this is Doctor Liz Heffron."

Sick butterflies began a drunken waltz in her belly and she clenched her fist to her stomach struggling for a normal voice.

"Yes, Liz." Her hand shot out and snatched up the handset. *Please don't . . .*

"Lauren, I won't waste your time, I know how anxious you are." Despite the woman's professional detachment, her voice dropped an octave. "The blood types match."

Lauren squeezed her eyes shut, disappointment evident in her sigh and slump of her shoulders. "Are you sure?" she asked, holding on to one final sliver of hope.

"I'm sorry, Lauren," she sighed.

"That's okay. It's not your problem. Thanks." Reckoning was upon her. It was true. Her daughter had a father.

Lauren replaced the receiver and cupped her hand to her mouth, imagining how she would break the news. Gathering her things, Lauren methodically straightened her desk with absent practice. There was no pleasure in the ritual because today that's all it was. The usual sense of accomplishment after a full day's work was usurped by stark reality.

The blinking and buzz of the phone delayed her progress as she tried to inject feeling into her voice.

"Hello, this is Lauren."

"Lauren, it's Eric."

Silence hung between them as thick as fog until she broke the quiet with, "Congratulations."

"Thank you."

Lauren could hear him struggling, his words broken and husky. He began to speak then stopped, then began again, only to end in silence. "Hell, I'm not making any sense."

Eric stopped, and she thought it was just as well. Her eyes brimmed with tears listening to him sigh and breath heavily. Somehow she had expected gloating, more fanfare, even a laugh of jubilation, but not this. Not a humbled man. This was too much.

She cleared her throat. "I'm leaving now. As soon as I get home I'm going to tell her." The words broke her heart. "S-shall we call you after?"

"I would appreciate that."

"Okay then, uh, see you later."

"Thank you, Lauren."

"You're welcome," she said to the silence. He had already hung up.

Lauren picked up her briefcase and shrugged into her coat. The clock on her desk chimed, and she stopped at the door to check the time. Shayla should just be getting home. She hurried back to the desk and dialed her house.

"Shayla, it's Mom. How are you, honey?"

"Fine," she said, sounding distracted.

"You got company?"

"Yeah, Malik stopped by."

"For what? Did Clarissa send him to pick up their Christmas gifts? Tell Malik to tell his nosy mother we'll see them Christmas Eve just like every year." Lauren tried to keep her voice light, but failed. Shayla didn't seem to notice.

"No, he came by to bring down the Christmas boxes from the attic. Ma, did you want something?"

"Yes, I don't have any more appointments for today and I thought we could spend the evening together. I've got something to tell you." Her voice dropped under the weight of its importance.

"Mommy, are you okay?"

Lauren smiled tenderly, knowing Shayla must be worried to call her mommy. "I'm fine, darling. I'll be home in an hour. Tell Malik I said hi."

"Okay, bye."

"I think that's it." Shayla surveyed the boxes with distracted interest. She was really focusing on Malik's biceps that flexed as he dropped the last box on the rug in the den. It popped open and she recognized the plastic bag full of handmade ornaments that her mother had accumulated over the years. Shayla turned away embarrassed when he picked up the bag.

"Ma's coming home, you gotta go." She tried to snatch the bag, but he held it, fingering the plastic, smoothing it over an angel she had made in the fifth grade. Her mother could be so stupid sometimes, keeping all this junk.

Shayla dropped her hands to her hips, and wondered how she was going to get a so-fine brother like him to recognize her. He handed her the bag.

"Did your mom want me to do something else?" The tall angular boy stood proud and handsome, arching his hand in a pretend jump shot. He held the pose and added the "Swish," sound before heading for the refrigerator. Shayla watched his smooth moves but crinkled her nose as he drank from the half gallon carton of milk.

"Use a cup." She lowered her chin to her hand as she sat on the stool by the counter. He wiped his mouth and replaced the container.

"Why? I never did before.

Shayla crossed her legs, hoping she had his undivided attention. When she looked into his eyes, she knew she did. It was now or never, she reminded herself, and gave him her most sexy smile. "I heard through the grapevine this friend of mine likes you." When his ears twitched with interest, and his eyebrow shot up, her heart pumped. Tingles shot through her when a handsome smile parted his lips. Tall like his mother and father, Malik walked over and leaned on one elbow on the counter in front of her.

"Who is she?"

"I'm not gonna tell you her name, but I'll describe her to you. She wants to keep it down low."

"Why she want to keep it on the D.L.? If she likes me, I'm gonna find out anyway."

"Do you want to know what she looks like or what?"

"Yeah," he said, his hands flowing expressively in front of him.

Shayla smiled and softened her voice. "She's short, and medium-brown skinned. She's got black hair."

"Long or short?"

"Short and she has gray eyes. She's cute," she added confidently.

"What school does she go to?"

"I can't say."

"Why?"

"Cause she don't want everybody in her business. You want to meet her?"

He contemplated for a moment and she held her breath praying. "Yeah, I'm down with that. Tell her to meet me at the skating rink Friday night. You think she'll come?"

"Yeah, she'll be there." Shayla suppressed her excitement as she walked him to the door.

"I gotta go. Peace." He looked curiously over his shoulder at her before getting in his car and backing down the driveway.

"Bye." A broad happy smile spread across her face. Yes! Yes! *It's me. It's me!*

Chapter Ten

Take it easy, Lauren warned herself as she walked into the house from the garage. She watched from the door, wanting to remember this moment forever. Just the two of them. Lauren stopped the trek down memory lane and walked up to Shayla and tapped her on the shoulder.

"I'm home."

"Hey, Ma. I didn't hear you come in." She turned off the compact disc player and laid down the headphones.

Lauren walked over to the neat desk and laid her coat over the chair and her briefcase by the wooden leg.

"We need to talk, honey. Let's sit down."

Shayla followed her mother to the couch and sat next to her. Lauren clasped their hands together. "Ma, I hope you're not about to jump on me about the other thing." Lauren shook her head filling her voice with false cheer.

"Shayla, what I'm going to tell you is a wonderful blessing. It's something I know you used to hope for a long time ago

and, well, it's come true. I just want you to know that I love
you with all my heart.''

"Ma, tell me. You're scaring me.''

Their eyes locked together and she said, "I know the identity
of your biological father.''

Shayla's mouth hung and Lauren's heart thundered. Eric's
eyes stared back at her making it more difficult to finish.

In a tiny whisper Shayla asked, "Who?''

"Doctor Eric Crawford.''

Shayla's hand gripped hers tight and seconds ticked by as
she squeezed her eyes tightly shut then covered her mouth with
her hands. A small scream escaped. Lauren drowned in the
wonder in her daughters lips.

A single tear streaked down Shayla's face breaking Lauren's
heart. Oh, God, she prayed don't take her away from me. "I
can't believe it, I can't believe it,'' she murmured the words
running together. She looked at her mother.

"Yes.''

Tears raced as Shayla began pacing, wringing her hands
nervously before she stammered, "How do you know this?
When? Oh, my God. I can't believe it. "Does he . . . does he
want to see me?''

Lauren rose, too. "Yes, he does.'' She held off the other
answers knowing they wouldn't register.

Suddenly Shayla reached for her mother, and Lauren caught
her in a fierce embrace. Their bodies shook with Shayla's sobs
and Lauren held her, loving her now more than ever before.
They stayed this way a long time. Lauren prayed Shayla would
never want to see him, knowing those prayers would not be
answered.

"When can I see him?'' Shayla's voice cracked tearfully.

"Honey, you don't have to see him right away.'' She gently
rubbed the tears from Shayla's eyes and kissed her cheek. "You
can take as much time as you like. But whenever you decide,

he wants to see you." At Shayla's surprised stare, she added, "When you're ready."

"Tonight?"

"Yes, if that's what you want."

Silence hung between them as Shayla struggled with the news. "I want to see him."

"Baby, are you sure you're ready for this?"

"Ma, I've wanted this all my life. I can barely remember LeShay, but I remember wishing for my daddy. You and Daddy Hank came instead, but I never stopped hoping my father would find me."

Her words crushed her mother's heart, but Lauren tried to smile through the pain. Selfishly she had hoped Shayla wouldn't want to see him.

"Shall I call or would you like to?" she asked over the loud cracking of her most vital organ.

Shayla summoned her confidence and met her gaze. "Yeah, I'll just listen in."

Lauren went to the phone in the kitchen and perched it on her shoulder. She extracted a card from her pocket and dialed. Eric answered on the first ring.

"Hello." His voice commanded a response and Shayla's eyes widened. Lauren immediately regretted letting her listen in and maneuvered the phone so only she could hear.

"It's Lauren Michaels, Doctor Crawford."

"Yes, Lauren. How are ... things?" he asked, his voice tight.

"Fine. Shayla would like to see you this evening if that's not too much trouble."

"I'm on my way." His voice was hurried and breathless when she hung up. She took Shayla's hand and squeezed. Poor girl. She looked absolutely terrified.

"He's on the way. Don't be afraid, darling. I've talked to him several times and he seems nice enough."

She wished she could believe the lie she'd just told. It wasn't that he didn't seem nice. Nice had nothing to do with the way she saw him. He was masculinely sexual, utterly handsome, and wore black better than a panther. No. Nice was not the word for him.

Upstairs in her room, Lauren took off her suit and hung it up. Dressed only in a lace camisole and panties, she straightened the already neat items on the dresser then sat on the bed next to Shayla. Gently she rubbed her back and noticed that her face had broken out with two hives. Nerves, Lauren thought as she comforted her. Damn him, if he ever hurts her.

"What do you know about him, Ma?"

"I know he's got a big family and that he's eager to meet you. Again. We never talked about how your physical went."

Shayla visibly shrank and Lauren was sorry she mentioned it. "Honey, we'll talk about it another time." She gave her a reassuring squeeze and moved to the closet.

The blue jeans and jeans top she selected were totally nonsuggestive, anti-sexual, and totally unappealing in any way.

But it wasn't him that she was worried about. It was her own reaction to him. So far her flowering attraction toward him was one-sided. And private. No one else knew and she had every intention of keeping it that way.

Good thing, she dutifully reminded herself, looking at her daughter, who chewed her nails off. I won't make things uncomfortable for her by not controlling myself, Lauren thought as she slipped her feet into high heels. This dowdy outfit was perfect.

Shayla ran and changed her clothes. Gone were the baggy jeans, replaced by a pair of not-so-baggy jeans and a clean top. Her short hair was brushed neatly and she had applied light gloss to her lips.

"He seems like a nice guy. Just give him a chance," Lauren reassured and wondered why she was suddenly rooting for him.

The doorbell sounded and they both froze. Lauren looked at

Shayla, then gathered her in her arms hugging her tight. "Come down when you're ready, okay?"

Shayla nodded and Lauren forced herself to walk down the stairs with a slow step.

"Hi, come in." She stepped aside, opening the door wide so Eric's broad shoulders could pass. His face struggled to maintain a calm composure. The light sheen on his forehead gave away his nervousness as did the silent overlapping of his fingers as his hand hung at his side. She was sure the move was unconscious, but it revealed his inner emotions.

"Shayla will be down in a minute. Why don't we sit in the den?"

He cleared his throat. "Okay."

Lauren led Eric through the living room, around the corner and into the den. They sat on the couch and she reached over and smoothed down the upturned collar on his shirt. Her hand rested briefly on his shoulder. "She's just as nervous as you are. Just relax."

He jumped at the feminine gesture then reached up, bringing her hand down in his. Their eyes met.

"I've already thanked you so often it seems inadequate for what you've done. I owe you a great debt. I promise to pay you back for all of this."

"You don't have to."

He nodded curtly and released her hand.

Boxes of Christmas decorations lay open on the floor. The bag of her favorite ornaments lay on top. Possessively Lauren saw interest flare in his eyes and she wanted to snatch the bag and run. Those were hers. They were a culmination of years of Shayla's elementary and junior high school Christmas art work. *He's going to steal that, too.* She eased herself away from the vile thought.

"What have you got there?" Lauren asked searching for any distraction. She motioned toward the bag that lay at his feet, then folded her hands in her lap.

"Oh, I brought pictures of everybody. I just thought it would make it easier in case we don't have anything to talk about."

"I see. Can I get you something to drink?" Lauren hoped to ease some of his nervous finger switching. Up until last week he was a swinging single man without responsibility. Now he was a father and hadn't a clue as to what to do. She could have felt sympathy for him, had she not felt so sorry for herself.

"No, nothing." Minutes ticked by and she looked around the den trying to see it from his eyes. Too feminine, she thought critically. The long couch had been reupholstered in a deep peach floral print, which added to the light, airy atmosphere of the room. Everything else screamed feminine comfort and she smiled. He's probably going crazy with all these flowers.

"Hi."

Lauren and Eric surged to their feet and an awkward silence ensued. Father and daughter stared at each other, with identical gray eyes filled with equal amounts of apprehension.

"Hello, Shayla." He stopped short of reaching for her. When she didn't move he dropped his arms and looked to Lauren for assistance.

Lauren kept her eyes riveted on Shayla's face and saw her move before Eric did. Shayla reached out and hugged him saying, "Hello, it's good to meet you. Really meet you this time."

Lauren slipped unnoticed into the kitchen, her eyes overflowing as were theirs. She watched from around the corner as Eric caught Shayla to him in a tight hug that bespoke so many things. Finally he pulled back and wiped her face with his large hands.

"The pleasure is all mine." They both sat down laughing and Lauren quieted her sniffles, hoping they couldn't hear from her inner depths, her soul mourning.

They were silent except for a few uncomfortable giggles from Shayla and chuckles from Eric as they sized each other up. So quietly, it could have shook the room, Shayla finally said, "Why didn't you come for me when I needed you?"

No amount of preparation could have prepared Eric for the loaded question. There it was. Guilt, accusation, hurt, trust, and sadness blended together in just a few words. He looked for Lauren but she had slipped away. He was on his own.

"I'm sorry." The words carried the emotions he felt to the surface. "Had I known you were on this earth, you would have been with me." He took her hand. "Shayla, I can't turn back the clock, but I'm here now. I promise I'll never leave you." He paused, tightening his fingers around hers. "I'd like for us to be friends." When she didn't say anything, he continued. "I know this is a lot to ask, but do you think maybe you can forgive me?" Having never had to beg for anything in his life, Eric was humbled. He wanted her to want him so bad he could taste it.

"I don't know," her voice rang with honesty and apprehension. "I might like to try to get to know you first. Maybe become friends," she responded hesitantly.

Eric nodded, disappointed, yet understanding. "That sounds good to me."

"Do you remember my mother?"

"Yes, I do."

Hesitantly she asked, "Can you tell me about her?"

He expected this and was prepared. "LeShay and I met in high school. She was beautiful, like you."

The compliment made Shayla smile, and he gave her the edited version. Omitted was the truth about LeShay's wild ways, replaced with loving remembrance. "I just wish I had known about you." He took her cold hand in his again.

"Do you really?" she whispered, her brimming with tears.

"Yes, with all my heart I wish I had."

"I have to tell you something."

"Go ahead." Eric released her from the tight embrace he had drawn her into.

"I love my ma, and I don't want to come live with you."

Eric laughed thinking of the den of iniquity he lived in. "Okay, I won't pressure you there." He met her direct look. "Shayla, I don't want you to think I'm going to try to change everything in your life. I don't want you to leave your mother. She's a wonderful person, and I appreciate everything she's done to make this happen." He squeezed her hand. "I want you to be where you're happy."

"Are you married?"

"No." He laughed again at her shift in conversation.

"Good, I'm glad."

"Why?" he asked surprised.

"Because, I don't want to have to deal with somebody else right now."

He was stunned by her honesty, but expected no less. After all, she was a teenager.

"Do you have other kids?"

"No."

"Family?"

"Yes. As a matter of fact"—he nervously reached toward his feet for the bag—"I have pictures, if you want to see."

"Maybe later."

He shrugged and brought his hand to his lap. After a few uncomfortable attempts, they started talking. Their talk evolved, into a discussion about school and grades. They shifted to music and movies, then his job and family. Eric was surprised to find Shayla wanted to study forensic medicine. He was greatly impressed at the colleges she'd applied to. "Have you ever thought of studying at Emory?"

"No. Once my ma and I saw how expensive it was, I applied to other, more affordable schools."

"Well, maybe your mom and I could talk about that, if that's where you want to go."

"Want to go? I *dream* of going there." Her excitement

touched him and he decided right then if he had anything to say about it, he would make sure her dream would come true.

Lauren peeked around the corner, trying to be inconspicuous. Surprisingly Eric's gaze sought hers and she held it for a moment before ducking back into the kitchen. Even though it was awkward for them, she still felt his power surround her and take her breath away. No matter what the setting, he still had control.

He and Shayla continued talking and she was impressed with his candid, sometimes funny answers. Her heart beat double time when Shayla called to her.

"Yes, darling?" she answered, her voice unnaturally high.

"Can we go over to his house for Christmas?"

Lauren stiffened as helpless anger swirled around her. He had already started moving in! That's my time, she wanted to scream. Time for Shayla to spend it with her . . . family.

The excitement in Shayla's voice stopped the "no" that lay between her teeth and tongue. Her daughter had just found her father and wanted to spend time with him. It would be cruel to say no now. Lauren felt burning defeat in the pit of her stomach. Frustrated, she held the cookie sheet in her hand and imagined it plastered over Eric's big head. Her lips curled into a satisfied smile and she calmed the fire that threatened to overflow. Lauren opened her mouth to accept, but was cut off.

"You're invited, too of course. Please say you'll come."

"I can't. My mother will be here. But Shayla can go," she said plainly. She walked to the open doorway between the den and kitchen and Shayla stared her down.

"Ma, I can't go without you and Grandma. Never mind, I'll stay here."

"No," they both chorused in unison.

Eric eyes silently begged Lauren to reconsider and she swam in the stormy gray sea. She resisted the urge to land the tray again, on his head.

"Lauren, please? We have more than enough. Everybody

will be excited to meet you. I won't exclude you.'' He had
risen and taken her hand in plea. His touch was warm and
comforting and his gaze beckoned her response. Lauren felt
herself responding to his touch and she shot a quick glance at
Shayla.

"Fine, we'll go.'' Lauren extracted her hand from his and
shook off the uncomfortable feeling she got from the odd
expression on Shayla's face. Father and daughter stood together
and once again she was excluded from their discussion. Slowly,
she walked from the room.

"What should I call you?'' Shayla asked.

Eric watched the beautiful face of his daughter and knew it
was too soon for her to call him what he longed to hear. "You
can call me Eric.''

"Are you hungry?''

"No, thank you. I could use a drink of water though.''

"I'll get it.''

"When does Christmas break start?''

"Tomorrow.''

"If it's okay with your mother, can I come by tomorrow
after work and spend some more time with the both of you?''

Irritation marked Shayla's tone. "We won't be here. My
grandma is coming in town and I have to go with her to
Geoffries Comfort Villa.'' Eric laughed when she stuck her
tongue out and scrunched up her nose. "Then we're going
Christmas shopping. And Friday my ma has to sing so it would
probably be too late for you to come over after she finishes
her set at Jimmy B's.''

"The supper club?''

"Yeah, she sings there every other Friday.''

Eric's thick brows knitted together at this discovery about
Lauren.

This news triggered an old memory. Her friend from the
food court had mentioned Lauren singing for all of the CNN
building to hear. He looked at her with new eyes. It was hard

to imagine that Lauren sang. These two were full of surprises. Somehow he felt forewarned. He needed to buckle his seat belt.

Reluctantly, Eric rose and they walked to the door. He rested his hand on the knob.

"Tell your mother I said thank you."

"She must have gone up to do some work. I'll get her. Ma!"

"No," Eric insisted, too late. "I don't want to disturb her any more today."

"I'm right here." Lauren descended the stairs.

Her daughter was suddenly shy. "He's getting ready to go. He wants to meet grandma and take us shopping Friday. You're not going to say no, are you?"

Shayla's voice tinged with challenge. Already he was dividing her family. Lauren met her daughter's gaze. "Of course not. But I thought you were going skating with Malik Friday."

"I am." Panic filled her gray eyes when she looked at Eric. "I can still go skating if we get back before seven."

Tension had tightened his shoulders, but he released it. "Deal." They shook hands and Lauren couldn't help smiling when they did. The first peal of the phone had Shayla tearing up the stairs. She turned halfway up.

"Don't leave yet. I want to say good bye."

"I'll be right here." Eric closed the door. He and Lauren watched their daughter go in her room and shut the door with a resounding thud.

Awkwardly she gazed at her bare toes and settled her arm across her stomach. "Why don't we sit and wait for her to finish," Lauren offered. "It may take a while."

"That's okay by me. I just enjoy watching her." They settled on the couch talking low. "How are you feeling?"

"Is that for a medical diagnosis?"

"No. Personal."

Lauren hoped she misinterpreted his meaning. Surely she was the only one with misplaced sexual attraction. She decided to be honest to a point. "I feel like I'm swimming in a big ocean and sharks are surrounding me."

He drew back surprised. "That bad?"

"Yes." she crossed her legs bringing them beneath her. "I'm glad you two hit if off. Really." Lauren's gaze gravitated to her daughters closed door. "Shayla's been wanting a father for a long time. You're her dream come true." She looked at him. "Please don't disappoint her."

Eric moved close, and took her hand. "I won't. Thank you."

She squeezed and tried to pull away. He held on. "For what?"

"For raising her."

Lauren whispered. "I didn't do it for you."

His after-shave tickled her nostrils with its woodsy, masculine scent. So appropriate for Eric. "I know. Lauren?"

"Yes?"

"You're beautiful." Lauren snapped her hand from his rising.

"Ma?" Guiltily she turned as her daughter came out of her room and leaned over the banister.

"Yes ... Yes darlin'?"

"Aunt Rissa wants to talk to you."

Lauren turned back to Eric who had risen also. What had they been thinking? Her gaze begged him to stay away from her. For the first time in a long time, she didn't know if her resolve would hold.

"I'd better get that. Goodnight, Doctor."

"Lauren?" She wanted to hate the way his mouth made love to her name, but couldn't. She had no choice but to face him. Her daughter was a witness. "My name is Eric."

She placed her foot on the next step and nodded. "Eric. Goodnight."

Shayla glided down the steps a mysterious smile on her face. It flattened when she stopped before him. "You're going to come over tomorrow, right?"

''Nothing would stop me.'' His daughter nodded and avoided his gaze. They'd all had a big night. Still, he hated to leave. ''Well, goodnight, Shayla.''

''Goodnight, Eric,'' she said hesitantly. He hoped it would get easier for her to say and would remain a delight to hear.

His heart swelled as he followed the pathway back to his car. Backing out of the driveway, he felt like a million bucks.

Rissa's voice filled her ear, but Lauren couldn't think of one thing worthwhile to say. She peeked out the blinds as she watched Eric walk down the lighted driveway to his fast car. He was smiling hard. Happy. Probably elated.

He backed the expensive machine down the drive and pulled away.

Lauren felt as if her world had shattered into one thousand pieces.

Chapter Eleven

Eric slipped the hostess a ten dollar bill when she sat them at the table behind an obscuring palm plant. It was exactly what he wanted. The dimness of the supper club also suited his purpose. He wanted to be as unobtrusive as possible. Eric sat down and snapped open the menu in front of his face, then yanked at his brother Michael's sleeve, who stood looking around.

"What's wrong? Why all the cloak and dagger?" Michael demanded before sitting down.

"Sit down. I don't want her to know I'm here."

Eric looked over the top of the menu and tried to appear casual as he spotted Lauren's friends at a table in the front.

The collar of his shirt suddenly felt two sizes too small. He inhaled deeply and focused on the menu.

"How did things go with Shayla yesterday?"

"Man, she's great." Eric beamed proudly. "Chaney, Lauren's mother, is a ball of fire, too. I think she and the family are going to hit it off right away."

"For the record," Michael adopted the same tone he used when making opening statements. "I think you're making a grave mistake. You shouldn't misjudge Shayla's mother. She says she doesn't want anything, but she could have you in court for years."

Michael's voice took on a urgency when Eric ignored him and continued to study the menu. "Why put yourself in the position where you're vulnerable?"

Because she did it for me. What kind of woman would turn her life upside down based on the word of a stranger? Their lives were irrevocably changed. He felt he owed it to her somehow.

"You're attracted to her," Michael said, with resigned certainty.

Eric fumbled with the menu, placing it on the table. He met his brother's gaze with a shake of his head.

"I'm something," he agreed. "I had to be here tonight to find out."

Michael hesitated, looking at him. He laid the cloth napkin on his lap, taking another approach. "What did the folks say when you told them?"

Eric scoffed, folding his hands as he remembered his mother's reaction. "You would have thought I announced my intention to move back into my old room and live with them forever."

"She was happy?"

"To say the least. She can't wait until Christmas day. She even told me not to buy her a Christmas present."

Eric nodded in the wake of his brother's disbelief. Everybody knew how much his mother liked gifts.

"She said I just gave her the best present since the birth of her last grandchild."

"What about Pop?" Michael asked incredulous.

"You know Pop. He told me to do the right thing and marry Lauren. He knows she isn't Shayla's biological mother, but he said he raised me to be responsible."

Eric felt the heat of his father's words surround him. It wasn't a half bad idea, but Lauren wouldn't go for a workaholic, ex-playboy for a husband, anymore than he could marry someone he didn't love. Not that marriage was even an option. It hadn't worked the first time according to Marie's diary. Round two probably wouldn't be much better.

"I told him I am doing the right thing. I'm going to take care of Shayla from now on."

"Then why are we here?" Michael asked with patient irritating logic. Eric stared at his brother and knew there wasn't one spontaneous bone in his body. What a shame for April.

He avoided the answer, uncertainty abounding. "Do you have somewhere else to go?"

"No."

"Then relax," he ordered, loud enough that the couple at the next table turned and stared at them.

The decision to come to the club tonight hadn't been a conscious, thought plan. He'd known he would come as soon as Shayla mentioned it. Getting to know Shayla would take years. Years he looked forward to with eager anticipation. But Lauren was another matter. There was something about her that made him feel urgent, hurried. Like a pressing question that needed an immediate answer. He wanted to know more about her. Now. From what he could gather from Chaney, Lauren worked hard, didn't date, travel, or have much fun. She raised Shayla and sang. She was pretty much a loner.

God, but she was beautiful. Incredibly sexy in her, faded jeans she'd worn the other day. She may have tried too hard to play down her natural sexiness, but the denim emphasized the rounded bump of her butt, the enticing swell of her breasts, and her tiny waist. Since then, he'd been in a state of semi-arousal. *That* was why he was here.

The waitress sashayed over and gave them her most dazzling smile. Michael ordered first, then Eric, who turned his attention back to the growing crowd that was seriously working on CP time. It was already a half hour past show time.

The waitress took the menu from his hand, and held it so it blocked Michael's face from view while she whisered in his ear "No, thank you." Eric and Michael chuckled at her less than enthusiastic departure.

Michael started in on him again. "She's available," he indicated the disappointed waitress with a nod in her direction. "Man, we can still leave before this blows up in your face."

"I'm staying," his tone was final. Michael threw up his hands, giving up.

Eric recalled Lauren's shaking hands and pained, beautiful eyes. She evoked something in him he'd thought long dead. Seeing her wasn't enough. He had to get this infatuation of her out of his system if he was going to see her every time he came to pick up Shayla. For his sake, Eric hoped she would be terrible tonight.

Hot chicken fettuccine and diet soda arrived just as the lights dimmed and cast the club into a fire glow.

Stabbing his fork into the hot noodles, Eric lifted it to his mouth. He burned his lip on the creamy white sauce and the fork thumped to the cloth table. Unprepared for her entrance, Eric and Michael stared, transfixed.

Lauren seemed to arrive on a cloud. She walked with a seductive casualness that had his senses immediately on alert. The gold, form-fitting top eased to an enticing point off her shoulders, just above her breasts. Accentuated with a flowing black and gold skirt, it willowed about her legs as she moved center stage. Her hair was bound with an African styled kofi, of black and gold, and it set off her almond-shaped eyes. One gold bangle bracelet encircled her wrist and matched the earrings that dangled from her small ears.

She looked like a beautiful African queen.

When she smiled and waved, her hazel eyes twinkled. The

responding applause lifted the expectant mood in the intimate club.

She joined her friends at the front table, talking with them, while the band members took their places. Her heart-shaped face brightened and her fiery red lips parted easily when she blew them a kiss.

"Hello," she addressed the crowd and thanked the stage hand for the microphone and her stool on which she perched her small bottom. "Merry Christmas. Happy Kwanzaa, and let's see, Happy Hanukkah." Everybody laughed.

"Tonight we're going to take it light. I was thinking of some Anita." She nodded, adjusting her bottom on the stool when people cheered.

"Maybe a little Sade"—she smiled at the increasing response—"and how about we wrap it up with some Whitney?"

The din of applause had Eric on the edge of his seat, bewitched. Her magic spell had already been cast.

The response of the crowd was mystifying, and she hadn't even hummed a note yet.

Then she did. And it was powerful.

Her voice filled the room with its strength and range. Eric felt it lift him off his seat, spin him around, then land him gently back within the protection of the dark swivel chair. Her multi-octave range moved over the hills and valleys of songs taking everyone within its reach back to church on some, and on others, making them feel as if they were outside in the warm, breezy Atlanta sunshine.

She scatted, oooh'd, hummed, and played until he was convinced she could do no more. The longer she sang, the larger need to be fulfilled became, and he could only think of one way to replenish himself.

Michael stared, enraptured, too. His food lay untouched. He was mesmerized by Lauren, who walked the stage, working the crowd. She had caught them in her silken net, and they were completely at her mercy.

She ended with a popular show tune, and the applause and appreciative whistles from within the small club were warm and generous. People yelled out one Christmas song in particular. When she looked as if she were considering it, they urged her by beating on the tables, cheering.

Eric watched expectantly, his curiosity peaked. She had sung for two hours and had given them her all. What more was there?

The crowd chanted while she consulted with the band, who were wringing wet with sweat. Lauren moved in front of the microphone, and the crowd applauded loudly. She curtsied low, and the club was plunged into total darkness. Above their heads, white lights twinkled like stars from the heavens and a hush fell over the audience. Gone were the sounds of clinking glasses, and idle chatter. The bustle of the staff stilled. Drink orders halted.

Everyone watched. Waiting.

Expectantly Eric looked on, then one golden light shone on Lauren. Her eyes were closed, arms raised, fingers splayed, quiet. The musicians waited and she sent a silent signal. Softly, the electric guitar was laid down, as were the sticks for the drums, and the piano man folded his hands in his lap. She was flying alone.

A cappella.

Her small hands folded around the microphone and her lips touched the foam covering, singing the first note so low, Eric missed its beginning. Deep in texture, he would have thought someone so small incapable of reaching that depth of range. But she did.

She sang from her heart about the birth of Christ, and heavenly peace, moving only with the cadence of the song and the pat of feet against the floor. The beat began slow and kept time for her vocal rhythms as she reached into herself for the spirit of the hymn.

Eric closed his eyes and believed in the words she sang. How powerful was her voice, making every nerve in his body soar as she moved through the chords, until she slowed and began to hum, finally ending it, letting him off the mighty ride.

The room was quiet for a moment, everyone was awestruck with her rendition of "Silent Night." Then one, far in the back, began to applaud. A wave of clapping appreciation followed, ending in an ovation.

Eric forgot his objective of keeping a low profile, and stood too, cheering with the rest as she bowed graciously and threw two-handed kisses to the audience.

"Happy Holidays." She laid down the microphone, picked up her water glass and left the stage. The door closed behind her and he still stood clapping. Eric wanted to take her in his arms and tell her how much she had changed his life. It wasn't just the song, or even today. It was her. From the day he met her, everyday of his past seemed the same. But the changes that had occurred to him since they met were enough to keep him spinning for years, and he knew it was due, in part, to her.

The room was heated, and moisture hung like dew in the air. Eric glanced around and took in Lauren's effect on strangers. There were tears in the eyes of some, while others hugged and kissed, offering best holiday wishes. All were reluctant to leave. Leaving meant the spell would be broken. People had come to see a show, and left with a part of Lauren. They, as he, would never be the same.

Eric slumped into his chair, feeling dissatisfied. Had Shayla not come out of her room at that moment the other night, would Lauren have kissed him? He had to see her. Rising, he dropped five twenties on the table. "Pay for dinner. If I'm not back in twenty minutes, leave."

He was gone before Michael could protest.

Chapter Twelve

"I'd like to see Lauren." Eric returned the cool stare of the big, dark-skinned, bald man that blocked a door marked, TALENT.

"Do she know you?"

"Yes, she does. I'm Eric Crawford." Eric held the man's gaze, unwavering, not about to let the hefty bouncer be what kept him and Lauren apart.

"Look, man," he said, several minutes into the standoff. "I'm her daughter's father and I really need to see her."

The bald man raised one eyebrow, but otherwise remained expressionless. He eventually shouted, "Lauren, do you want to see Eric Crawford?"

The door slid open and Lauren's head peeked out. Her perceptive hazel eyes reflected her discernment of the contest between the two men who still glared combatively at each other.

"What are you doing here?"

"I came to see you." Her eyes widened and he melted when

her hand fluttered to the jade stone around her neck and clutched it.

"Do you want me to get rid of him?"

"No, thank you, PeeWee. Come in." Eric stepped past the man and walked inside. He glanced around the tunnel—like room and wondered how anyone could dress in this closet. One chair, a small vanity table, and mirror filled all the space and he turned in the spot where he stood to face her. The gold flecks in her outfit reflected against the muted light and he took one step forward.

If I touch her now I won't want to stop. If I don't touch her, I'll die. Coins tinkled when he withdrew his hand from his pocket. *I'll die a happy man.* He took her hand. Her eyes remained locked on their hands as he lifted them. Mahogany lashes fluttered, then closed when he pressed her fingertips to his lips. He released her hand, slid his deep into his pockets.

They smiled at each other. "Why are you here, Eric?"

His tone was gentle, but matter-of-fact. "To confess how much I'm attracted to you. I have been since I first saw you. You amazed me tonight. Your voice is beautiful."

She smiled shyly and he said, "I want to finish what we started the other night." Eric took another step. Lauren matched it.

"And what was that?"

He reached for her. "To kiss you." He wanted to pull her closer, to lean into her and claim her sexy mouth. But she had to want him too.

With his chin he nudged aside her bangs, getting used to the feel of her against him. The tip of his finger glided across her face and when she began to squirm, he lifted her chin. Her breathing quickened.

"Will you scream for your bodyguard if I kiss you?"

Red sparks flashed in her eyes and she parted her lips.

"No . . . No. I won't scream."

Eric dropped his mouth to hers and claimed it. Possessively, hungrily, her supple lips glided with his. Mating their tongues, Lauren accepted his thrusts by returning the sensuous motions. His fingers tightened on her jaw and he dragged his mouth from hers. "Lauren, I want you."

She wrapped her arms around his neck, and he cupped her bottom, bringing her higher in a divinely slow, tortuous motion. "I like the sound of that."

Permission granted, their mouths latched again and he groaned, desiring her, pressing her into him once more.

Her response was light and breathy sighs, that almost undid him. She was such a feather-weight. Eric raised her high enough balancing her against him with one hand. They both watched as he reached between them and freed one breast from the gold top. The darker center grew taut under his palm and he couldn't stop when his thumb gripped the underside of it. He had to taste it. Eric wasted no time covering the pointy nipple with his mouth.

Her thighs gripped his sides and he took a step back and landed on the chair. He captured the hardened peak between his teeth and tongue and licked the underside of it. He laved it again and again until the small bud blossomed to a desert bloom. In her excitement, Lauren's pleasurable cries made him want to please her more.

He braced her back with his hands, stroking over her heart with his tongue. She squealed one long high peal, that could have been mistaken for a sung note. But he knew the deal. It was the passion call. He waited until her heartbeat slowed, then claimed her other breast with the same rapaciousness.

The gauzy fabric of her skirt overflowed his hands as he lifted the sides, seeking her rounded bottom.

Eric straddled her over his knee and slid his hand to her center. "Don't scream," he warned, when he stroked beneath the thin fabric.

"Ahh," she groaned aloud, losing the rest of her murmurs in his mouth.

"Don't." He stopped. Praying. "Don't, don't . . . stop," she chanted, holding him tight, lost in the oblivion of passion. Eric found the moist garden and slid his finger inside. He stroked in and out, his other hand pressing her forward. Gently he withdrew. Her mouth fell beside his, she whispered, "Help. Me. Come."

His thickened desire threatened to explode and he pushed her moistness against his dryness and struck the sensual chord again.

Lauren's teeth closed on his neck and pleasure, pain, and warm rain filled him.

Eric had no idea how long her climax lasted but he was glad he hadn't died before seeing it. His hand jerked with her spasms, his elbow hitting the table.

"Lauren, you okay?" PeeWee's bark halted their heated lovemaking. Eric let her kiss swollen lips go and wrapped his arms protectively around her. "Are you okay?" he asked, a small smile parting his lips.

Their gazes locked. Embers of desire still burned in their depths. "No," she said weakly.

"Tell him how you feel."

She had regained some of her composure and looked with a glazed expression toward the door. "I'm fine, PeeWee."

Her face lingered on his shoulder, then her composure started to return. "Oh, no." She stood up, then staggered. Her eyes darted at her near nakedness and his wet fingers. "Oh, my God," she whispered. "Oh, my God. What am I doing?"

"Lauren—"

"No!" She clutched her bare breasts and then turned around pulling up her top in one swift motion. "I must be crazy," she muttered, shooting him with accusing glances over her shoulder.

"Lauren, we're grown. I don't answer to anybody and I'm not attached. I didn't think you were attached, either."

Eric wanted her back in his arms so badly, he physically ached. But mostly, he didn't want her to regret what had just taken place between them. Her cheeks were flushed and her eyes reflected brilliantly. Pain wracked them.

"I'm not. But—" She half turned, with her hand in the air to silence him. Her eyes were closed tight. "I don't let my physical emotions control my logical responsibility."

Nervously she finger combed her hair, trying to restore herself to her former sheltered demeanor. She fidgeted with her clothes, erecting walls to separate them. She turned away, sucking in her breath, when he withdrew a handkerchief from his pocket, wiping his hand. She couldn't shut him out. He needed her. Needed her to at least acknowledge what just happened.

Eric's blood rushed through his veins like Niagara Falls as he eased her around to face him. He rested his chin on top of her head.

"You're physical emotions are just fine to me." With great satisfaction, he held her up when her knees buckled. "It's the illogical emotions that are keeping a perfectly healthy woman from experiencing a natural desire to have her affection returned."

Lauren's shoulders went back, her chin up. She stepped away from the support he offered.

"I . . . I have responsibility." Insecurity clouded her eyes.

"I'm not into casual sex. My primary goal has always been to see my daughter raised in a happy, healthy home. Now that she's found you, she'll be more emotional and I have to be there for her. If it weren't you, Eric, it might be different." She pointed at him.

"You and I can't have a sexual relationship. We can't have a relationship at all. We have to think of Shayla."

"Tell me the truth. What do you feel in here?" His fingers heated her breast bone. "Not here." He pointed to her head.

"I . . . I have responsibility."

Eric shoved his hands in his pockets and closed his eyes. How could he make her see she could have both? He opened his eyes and gazed at her. "Who hammered it into you that having adult feelings and acting on them wasn't responsible?"

"Nobody! I know what is right and what isn't. Shayla comes first, Eric."

"And what if you want to have an adult relationship?"

"No!"

"Why?" he backed her up so that she had nowhere to go. "Tell me what it felt like, Lauren." He lowered his voice and waited. Losing control wouldn't make her reveal what lay hidden inside her. She had to let it out herself.

"Good," she whispered. Her voice grew stronger. "It feels good to have you touch me. Are you happy now?" Anger filled the hazel pools.

Something was wrong here. Eric pursed his lips, searching for what it was.

He stared at her long and hard then gathered her to him.

"No," she protested. "We're not going to repeat that. It can't happen again."

He said nothing and held her until she quit fighting the invisible monster she struggled with. Then gently, he cradled her in his arms.

What would stop a desirable, attractive woman from having a relationship, casual or otherwise? Especially a woman as responsive as she. He couldn't stand to think of her with anyone else though.

Eric took a stab in the dark following an instinct. "I don't think this is just about Shayla. You're using her to protect yourself from something else." He ran his hand up and down her spine, feeling her bones melt against his fingertips. "I'm not him, Lauren."

"Don't go there, please." Her muffled voice came from the middle of his chest. "We have to forget this ever happened."

"I can't." He made her look up at him. "Can you? Can you forget this?" He pressed her hand over his racing heart and placed his over hers. The beats mimicked each other. "Was it worth forgetting?"

"No, it wasn't." Her voice trembled.

"What kind of relationship will we have, platonic or otherwise if we can't look each other in the eye?"

"Eric, I'm tired. I just want to go home."

"I'll take you." He grabbed her coat slinging it over her shoulders. "Come on."

"Where?" she asked in a low exasperated voice.

Eric splayed his hand in the center of her back and propelled her out the dressing room door. "We're going to talk on the way."

PeeWee eyed them with feigned boredom. Eric could tell by the way he clenched his fists, he'd heard everything that had gone on behind those doors. He met the man's gaze directly. There was nothing he could do about it now. He extended his fist to the man who pounded it with his own.

"Later. Remember me. I'm going to be around."

PeeWee shot him with his finger and Eric took Lauren's arm. He guided her down the hall, through the back door, and into the cold night.

There weren't many places open at one in the morning, so he had to think fast. Spotting Michael at his car, he steered Lauren toward hers. "You mind if I drive?" She handed the keys over without protest.

Eric adjusted the seat and wheeled her car in the opposite direction of her house. Lauren sat in the seat staring out the window.

"This isn't the way to my house."

"I know. I told you we're going to talk and we are. Shayla and Chaney are home, so we can't talk there." He picked up the car phone and dialed a three digit code. "Tell her you went out with some friends and you're going to be a little late."

"No. I'm not going to lie to my daughter to please you.

Take me home." Lauren refused the extended phone and stared at him.

"Have it your way. I'll tell her myself." He raised the phone to his ear.

Lauren grappled the receiver from his hand and put it to her ear just as Shayla answered.

"Shayla, honey, you asleep?" There was silence. "Yeah, that was a dumb question. Look, I'm going to be a little late. How late?" Lauren raised her eyebrows and met Eric's gaze. He held up two fingers.

"A couple of hours. Go to bed, honey. I'll see you in the morning. Goodnight."

Lauren replaced the receiver and crossed her arms over her chest. They rode in silence for a long while as the highway unfolded before them. Eric watched the road, keeping the car at Atlanta's comfortable speed of seventy.

He exited, turning west.

"We have nothing to talk about. What happened tonight was unfortunate. I accept full responsibility." He didn't want to hear that. She felt their pleasure just as much as he did. That's what had her running scared. He didn't respond. Silence fell.

Eric turned the car into a space outside a beige brick building and stopped. "Where are we?" she asked suspiciously.

"At the center." Determined not to be sidetracked, he unlatched her seat belt and opened his door.

"My keys, please," Lauren said, as he slid them into his pocket.

"Come on, Lauren." His actions were focused. He circled the car and held her door open. She had no choice but to follow him into the building, shivering in the cool wind. Once again, he was having his way.

The center surprised her. It was homey and comfortable, designed as a place to learn but also as a place where family was foremost. Every wall was covered with photos of various versions of families.

Lauren stopped to closely observe one picture in particular. It caught her heart. Eric held a teeny, tiny baby in the palm of his hands. He wore hospital blues, his curly hair covered by a gauze skull cap. Beneath his chin was a rumpled mask. But what kept her eyes riveted was the way he gazed at the baby and the glisten in his eyes.

"He didn't make it."

"Oh, I'm so sorry." She choked on the lump in her throat, as she turned toward him. Lauren wanted to caress the deep grooves that sliced through his forehead but she kept her hands still.

"Most often, we're blessed and can save them. Sometimes, not." Eric took her hand, guiding her to a back cubicle. She wasn't sure if he were aware of the current of electric energy that flowed between them, but she couldn't ignore it. It intensified, tenfold when he touched her. He sat behind a gray desk, staring up at her. Lauren wiped the tears from her eyes, frowning in surprise.

"You don't have an office?"

"This is it." He pivoted in the small space as he spread his arms wide. "We're here to get a job done. I'm not here enough to need more space. Although I wish I were."

"Really? Why?" Lauren absently kicked off her shoe and sank into the guest chair, sitting on her foot.

Eric smiled. "Because somebody has to keep programs like this in our community or we would drown in the muck of our own situations."

"And you're that person?"

"I do what I can." He opened a miniature refrigerator and pushed a bottle of fruit juice toward her. He waited for her to set the bottle down, then leaned back, balancing the chair on two legs.

"Tell me about Hank."

Lauren sighed. "What do you want to know?"

"What kind of husband was he?" His quick, cut-to-the-chase approach left her momentarily speechless.

"He was demanding, bossy, manipulative, hard-headed, and controlling. If we had lived in an autocratic society, he would have been in his element. Anything else?" She rose from the seat limping high on one heel, then down on her bare foot around his tiny office space.

"How did you meet?" How did you fall in love?"

He could touch her frustration, it was so real. The way her chest rose and fell, took him back in time to hours ago, when he'd made it happen. A rush surrounded him as she breezed past him, her hand sliding along the back of his chair. Her fingernails grazed his neck and he resisted the groan that rose in his chest. Her voice brought him back to her.

"We met in college. I was a junior when we finally got together. He was serious, and I was convinced that I needed a serious man. He was so focused. I admired that. I wanted it." She turned to look at him.

"I thought seriousness was the mark of a grown-up. Someone who was above laughing at the common joke. Hank and I were like that. We were serious." She balled her fist and pounded her hand. "He was an accountant and I was an accountant. We would make lots of money by the time we were forty-five and retire to Florida."

Eric frowned. "To do what?"

"I don't know. Die I guess," she said, sarcasm curling her lips. "We didn't have a clue. We fell in comfortable. You know what that is?"

"Tell me." She didn't need much urging to say what he already understood about her.

"It's what happens when you don't dream anymore. When you settle." Lauren sank back in the chair and picked her perfectly polished nails. She picked until there was a chip in the enamel on her index fingernail. She stared at it a moment then balled her hand into a fist and placed it in her lap. "I didn't realize until he was gone that I hadn't lived. Hadn't seen or done anything. That's why you and I can't be together.''

"I still can't accept that." She met his gaze directly.

"Despite the fireworks," her gaze wavered, her cheeks coloring. "Despite . . . all that, I want . . . more.''

When she looked back, he knew what "more" was. It hit him like a ton of bricks and he was surprised that her pain and desires ran deeper than even he imagined.

Chapter Thirteen

"You've never been in love before."

From her expression, he knew he'd hit the bull's-eye.

"No, and I never will be."

"Why?" Eric challenged, wonder washing over him. "Scared?"

"I'm not scared of anybody."

"But you're afraid of something. Aren't you the least bit curious? Why can't you admit that you might like to try it?"

She seemed to gain resolve. Her hands stilled and she cocked her head to the side. "What is your fixation on my love life for? Besides, why should I tell you anything? You weren't successful at love. How would you know anything?"

Eric was quiet for a moment.

"I didn't mean to hurt your feelings," she said regretfully.

"You didn't." Eric waved off her apology. "I've had bad relationships. My wife died wanting to divorce me. But I'm not afraid to get it right the next time." He held her gaze and lifted her juice to his lips and drank. When there was just enough left for her to get one last swallow, he held the bottle to her lips.

He raised one eyebrow and studied her closed lips. "Do you have something I should know about?" Purposely he kept the glass there waiting for her answer.

Her hair skated over her shoulders when she shook her head. "Me either. Drink."

Lauren opened her mouth and drained the juice from the bottle. Eric lowered the glass resisting, claiming her sweetened, wet lips. "Something tells me there's more. You gave up singing." Eric guessed that a clap of thunder wouldn't have shook her more than his words did.

"I thought it was the right thing to do," she snapped, picking her nails again.

"Because he wanted you to." Eric pressed, knowing he was so close to the truth of her heart. He lowered the legs of the chair, leaning forward, leaving little room between them.

"Because I wanted to," she insisted, avoiding his gaze, her eyes trained on her hands.

"Because he wanted you to." Eric saw years of protection unravel before his eyes. Her expression was helpless, then red sparks ignited like fiery embers in her eyes.

"Yes!" She slammed her hand on the desk, staring at him. "Because he wanted me to! Because he wanted children right away and responsible women didn't sing. He wanted the marriage of Ozzie and Harriet. She didn't sing."

"He wanted children. What about you?"

"I wanted them, too. So . . . badly." He drew back, sorry he'd pushed. The ache in her voice bespoke her desire. But they had no children besides Shayla.

"What happened? Why did you adopt?"

"We didn't find out for years after the wedding that Hank was sterile." Her finger rubbed the desk in mindless circles. "We were devastated." The look in her eye was pain ravaged. "I wanted children so badly, I went to an attorney and inquired about adoption the next day. A short time later, we got Shayla. Two months later Hank was dead from a aneurysm.''

"I'm sorry.'' Her hand lay on the desk and he laced his fingers with hers. In the semi darkness, he couldn't tell where hers began and his ended. Yet, hers held vitality and braveness so large it amazed him that they weren't bowed from the pressure of being a single parent.

Thank you for raising my daughter. I love you for loving her. I love you.

"You don't have to do it alone anymore. I'm here. You can do whatever you want to do.''

"I know.'' Her disentanglement of their hands signaled the end of their shared silence.

"Because you're free,'' he said, guessing the direction she was heading. His stomach knotted. He wasn't included.

"That's right.''

"I want you.'' Once he said the words, a two-year weight lifted off his shoulders. Lauren had felt something tonight. Was it enough for her to try?

"I know. It won't happen.'' She stood and slid her arms into her coat. "Eric, it's late and I'm tired. I want to go home.''

For the past two years, he'd done more soul searching than he cared to remember. If he knew one thing, it was himself. Eric knew he wouldn't give up. "Let's go.''

Lauren fell asleep on the ride to her house. He used the time to think about Shayla and her mother and the impact they were having on his life. He'd never felt more settled, and unsettled at the same time.

The garage light didn't come on as he pulled onto Lauren's driveway, but Eric didn't mind. The moon lit the darkness and he took a moment to have her all to himself.

He brushed her face with his knuckle.

"Thank you.'' She unlatched the door and stepped out. "You drove me home. Where's your car?''

He smiled when she did and his heart flipped. "I hate to do

this, but I have to borrow your car to get home. I'll bring it back tomorrow."

"Okay. Goodnight." Her voice was so small, so cool.

"Lauren?" She turned and looked at him, her brows creased. "I'll be here early Sunday."

"Sunday?"

"Christmas Day." He reminded her with a slow grin. Eric reached out and freed the dangling earring from her coat collar. She touched her hand to his. "We'll meet you." Her mouth said what her eyes couldn't hide. "For Shayla's sake, let's just be friends."

"I would be lying to you and myself if I said that I didn't want more. I'll be here at noon." He added, "Don't be late."

"I'm never late." Lauren raised her chin and gave him an indignant stare.

"Great, then we shouldn't have anything to worry about. Dress casually." He helped her out of the car and followed her around the bushes to the front door. Eric opened it and she walked in.

"Lauren," he whispered, taking hold of her arm. For a moment he feared she would bolt inside and slam the door in his face. But she didn't. She turned and kept her head down.

"Yes?" He didn't plan what he was going to say, it just fell from his lips.

"I'll be thinking about you for the rest of the night. Dreaming of you next to me. Of me buried deep inside you." He drew her closer until their chests brushed. "I'll be imagining the taste of your breasts, and your heat . . ." he sucked in a breath his desire increasing. "And the warm rain," he whispered softly, his hands searching out her skin beneath her coat. When he reached her, she was burning. "I can't wait to have you stretched out beneath me, and watch you come again and again. Your squeals will be full-blown screams." Her forehead landed against his chest with a thud.

"I won't be able to resist if you keep this up."

Eric withdrew his hands from her back, purposely closing her coat. But he kept her close. The cold December air puffed from her lips in fast gasps. I'm hoping so. So rest for both of us, because if I close my eyes, I'll be dreaming about you. Goodnight, beautiful. Sleep well.''

Eric disappeared around the bush, started her car and drove away.

Tendrils of pleasure shot through her and Lauren rested her head against the door. Once she gathered the strength to walk up the stairs to her room, she slowly peeled off her clothes and lay down on the cold sheets.

Wide awake. *What am I going to do now?*

Lauren stared past the twinkling Christmas tree, her thoughts a million miles away. The glass of egg nog Rissa had pressed into her hand long ago sat untouched as questions about Eric swirled around her. He had been the talk throughout Christmas Eve dinner and even now, two hours later, everyone still wanted to know something about him. Lauren felt pressure rising again.

Escaping into the kitchen, she breathed deeply and wiped cornbread dressing off the counter. Filling the sink, she didn't turn when she heard the kitchen door open. Dishes slid past her hand into the sudsy water. "Hiding out?"

"No."

Rissa stood beside her and stilled her moving hands.

"What happened last night when he came to your dressing room?"

"You saw him at the club?" Lauren stared at her friend and felt nauseous. Her head started to ache and she blotted her wet hands on the dish towel. She had hoped to wipe that incident from her mind. But here it was twenty-four hours later and she could still feel the imprint of his mouth on her breast. She turned away.

"I saw a very determined man reaching out to you."

Rissa's long arm hugged her shoulders as she led the way to the breakfast area of the kitchen. They sat next to each other at the glass table and Lauren said quietly, "We almost made love in that tiny room." She looked up to see understanding in Rissa's eyes.

"I was so hot for him . . . It's never been like that before." An involuntary shudder made goose bumps jump out on her arms.

Rissa spoke compassionately. "That's good. It's been too long in coming."

"No, it can't happen." Lauren shook her head adamantly. "Did you see Shayla out there?" Her eyes widened expressively. "My father this, my father that," she mimicked. "I can't allow myself to get involved with him. It would be too much for her to handle."

"You're a grown woman with needs. I think you should go for it." Holding up her hands, Rissa warded off her objections. "I know for a fact it's been years since you've let anyone this close to you. He's the perfect candidate. He's Shayla's father. He's got a good job." She ticked his attributes on her fingers. "And he wants you, too. Honey, you've got the best of all worlds."

Lauren felt miserable.

"The things he said . . . This is going to blow up in our faces."

"Not if you don't let it. You need to deal with Shayla now and forget the rest of the mess."

Lauren half-listened remembering how patient he had been as they sat in the darkness of the center. He'd learned her secrets. What would that power do to him?

He hadn't even taken advantage of her when he could have. God knows, all he had to do was touch her there, one more time. Instead he let her go, but kept her up all night with his promising words. He had the power. She had never dealt with a man whose ego was strong enough to handle her strength, too.

Rissa's voice skidded into her thoughts. "Was it good?" Lauren squirmed, warming. His hands. Those wonderful hands. "Like I've never felt before. I wanted him so bad, I scared myself."

Rissa nudged her leg, smiling a knowing smile. "It would be nice to have a doctor in the family."

"Oh, please," Lauren moaned.

"Diva, you're your own woman. Stop worrying about Shayla for a change. And worry about how you're going to feel growing old. Alone."

Lauren massaged her head at the temples easing the aching pressure, seeing the wisdom in her best friend's words. She rose from the chair and smoothed out the cherry red skirt that covered her legs almost to the knee.

"So what did you get me for Christmas?" she asked changing the subject.

"A wish," Rissa replied and opened the door to the family room where everyone waited impatiently. It was time to open the presents.

"For what?" Lauren followed, the swinging door swaying back toward her.

"To get a man by the end of the year. Merry Christmas."

Lauren sat at the end of the sofa watching the interaction between Shayla and Malik. They were flirting! Watching them hold hands, Lauren swallowed. They had held hands before. They grew up together. But today was different somehow. Ever since they had gone skating a couple of weeks ago, Malik had called several times. And each time, Shayla would take the phone to her room and shut the door with a resounding thud.

Lauren suddenly recalled that when Malik had given Shayla the Christmas present from his family, he pecked her on the lips. Everybody ooh'd and Rissa shushed them, proclaiming their childhood innocence.

Shayla didn't just kiss people. "Shayla?"

"Yeah, Ma?"

"Come here for a minute." Lauren waited as she gave the video games to Malik, then pulled her off to the side.

"Is something going on between you and Malik?"

Tension squared Shayla's shoulders and she looked at the floor. "No."

Flustered for a moment, Lauren rethought what she had seen. Accepting Shayla's word, she rubbed her arm. "I was just wondering, honey. We're going to be leaving soon okay?"

"All right." Lauren noticed how she followed closely behind Malik as they went up the stairs. She tried to convince herself to believe. What? Her eyes or her heart? Contrary to what Shayla said, they were too stiff. Too formal. Until the kiss. Then it dawned on her.

Lauren sat bolt upright.

Could Malik be the one who prompted her to ask for birth control? Ever since their initial discussion, whenever she brought up the subject, Shayla claimed she didn't want to talk about it. She said the situation was over. But was it? Lauren abruptly marched up the stairs to Malik's door. Opening it without knocking, she was relieved and embarrassed to see the two sitting on the floor staring at the television, their fingers working the video controls with lightening speed trying to defeat each other.

"Aunt Lauren, come watch me kick Shayla's butt."

Thank God. These were kids she knew. "In your dreams, boy," Shayla responded and pressed the button shooting several times. His man flickered, losing life, and Lauren backed out of the room.

"No thanks, darlings, have fun. Shayla, we're leaving in ten minutes. Okay?"

"I heard you the first time," she said, her voice snotty, not looking at her mother.

Lauren shut the door and retraced her steps feeling foolish.

Chapter Fourteen

Malik rushed to the door and cracked it open watching Lauren's retreating back. He leaned against the door jamb relief apparent in his sagging shoulders.

"That was too close for me," he said after he closed the door and sat back on the floor next to Shayla.

"How could you tell someone was coming?" she asked, putting on more lip gloss.

"I have the hall rigged so that when you pass a certain spot the light over the door flashes."

"Your father and mother don't know?"

"Yeah, my pops does, he helped me put it in. But my mom doesn't," he said, drawing her back into his arms. "Where did you learn how to kiss?"

"I don't know," Shayla replied shyly, enjoying his touch.

"Well, I like it." He lowered his lips to hers again. He drew away and studied her face. "What's up with you and your moms? You've been treating her like shit."

"What are you talking about?" She scooted on her butt to

get away from him. Shayla crossed her arms over her chest and lifted her chin in the air defiantly.

"I don't know. You tell me. She do something?"

"Yeah." Shayla exploded. "She's always in my business. I don't have any privacy, she wants to control every part of my life and . . ."

"What else?" Malik gently prodded, when she broke off.

"I don't know . . ." How could she tell him she thought her mother was moving in on her father. The very idea made her sick to her stomach. Shayla pushed the thoughts away and moved closer. She turned her face up and ran a finger along his jaw. "I'm not worrying about her right now. Look what I've got." From beneath the bed she pulled a few sprigs of mistletoe.

Malik took the greenery from her hand and tossed it away. "We don't need that." He ducked his head and claimed her lips again.

Lauren sat beside her mother and kicked off her shoes. Relaxing to the Al Green Christmas CD, she heaved a sigh.

Her relationship with Shayla hadn't improved. She could tell she hadn't helped it any from the frosty glare Shayla gave her upstairs.

"Mama, did I get moody when I was Shayla's age?"

"Honey, you got moody. Then I got moody." Chaney laughed. "Sometimes your daddy would call before he came home to see if it was safe. He didn't want us to have one of his guns cocked and ready to blow him away if he walked through the door at the wrong time."

Lauren's lips curved in a half smile. She missed her father especially now at the holidays. She could always count on him to make things right for her.

"Mama, everything is going to be all right isn't it?" she asked, needing her mother's reassurance.

"Everything is just fine," Chaney said quietly. "Why haven't you talked to me about Shayla's father?"

"You met him didn't you? I figured you would want to draw your own conclusion about him."

"Well that's funny. I thought you were my daughter." Chaney rubbed her hands then gathered them into hers holding them tight. "Honey, your father wasn't supposed to steal my heart either. But one week after I met him, I was in love, ready to commit myself to him forever." She smiled, leaning closer. "I never regretted it."

"That's not what's going on Mama." Lauren corrected herself at her mother's reproachful look. "Well, I don't want it to. It'll only complicate an already complicated situation."

"I don't see what's so complicated. Are you more concerned about your feelings or Shayla's?"

"Both, Mama. Shayla's most importantly." Lauren recalled their explosive discussion from days ago and her earlier suspicions about her and Malik. Something didn't fit, but she couldn't put her finger on it. Obviously.

Her concentration hadn't been the same because of him. His lips seemed to touch her face at that moment. Lauren pulled her hands from her mother's and turned away.

"Aunt Lauren, you okay?" Her head snapped up and she looked into Amanda's eyes. Lauren lowered her hand from her cheek and balled it in her lap. Go away, Eric, her brain pleaded. She cleared her throat. "Yes, honey, I'm fine. Where's Donna?" Amanda rolled her eyes.

"You know her and Allen. They're off somewhere. Kissing," Amanda shivered, causing Chaney and Lauren to burst out laughing. Chaney patted the seat next to her and indicated for Amanda, Donna's daughter, to sit down.

"How's my second granddaughter?"

"Fine," she replied, returning Chaney's hug.

"Mandy, do Grandma a favor and go tell Shayla I need a hug."

"Okay, Grandma Chaney, we'll be right back." Amanda took the stairs two at a time. In the hallway, she closed the linen closet door but not before knocking down a handful of towels. Bending to retrieve them, she noticed the faint beam of light. The store she worked in had the same sensors for security. Carefully, she stepped over the light and opened the door to Malik's room with a rush, startling the kissing couple. "Oooh, I'm telling."

Malik and Shayla jumped apart, guilty expressions on their faces. "Shut up and close the door," Malik hissed and got off the bed.

"You might want to leave it open. It's kind of steamy in here."

"What do you want, Amanda?" Malik said, quickly standing: Both girls stared wide eyed at the prominent bulge in the front of his pants. Amanda sat beside Shayla on the bed. "Grandma wants a hug and kiss from her chaste, good girl, granddaughter."

Reaching for the remote and the hand controller, Amanda reset the video game and started to play. "I wonder what she's going to say when I tell her Shayla she can't come right now, she's kissing somebody else."

Malik landed on Amanda first holding her hands above her head while Shayla tickled under her arms. Laughing, and pleading, Amanda kicked and bucked unable to get away from the pair. "Okay," she yelled, breathing quickly. "I won't tell, I swear." She rolled away from them and stood. "You two make me sick. Come on, Shayla."

Shayla walked to the door, giving Malik a flirting glance as she brushed past him. "Bye, Malik."

"Later." His smile was soft and attractive.

Both girls walked down the hall and Amanda stopped Shayla at the top of the stairs. "You sure you want to get involved with him? I heard he's got a reputation."

"Amanda, you don't even live in this state, so how could you hear that?"

"I'm moving back with my mother and Allen. But I heard it at the movies last night. I saw him with some girl."

Shayla stared at Amanda stung by her words. Hiding her hurt feelings, she said, "Do you know who she was?"

"Nope. Just a light-skinned black girl, with long hair."

"I don't care, we're not together." At Amanda's look, she went on, "yet."

"Just watch it," Amanda warned. "I like Malik, but he's just like all the boys our age. He's just interested in what he can get from you." They started down the stairs and walked to the entry of the den.

"You're not going to tell are you?"

"No. Just watch your back." They entered the den and Shayla embraced her grandmother.

Once again, Lauren got a frosty look from Shayla, but she was too engrossed in her own thoughts to comment. She walked to the living room bay window and was joined by Rissa and Donna. "It's time for us to go." The words held a note of finality. Soon they would be facing Eric's family. The unsurity of it had her stomach in knots.

Her friends didn't let her down. They embraced her offering their love and support. Lauren's eyes shined when she stepped away. "Thank you," she whispered, struggling not to cry.

"Try to have a good time tomorrow," Rissa said after they got in the car. Everyone laughed when Chaney piped in, "We will."

They waved as they headed up the street and Lauren wished she could have her mother's easy spirit. Chaney started to sing one of her favorite Christmas songs as they drove home. "Joy to the World." Her voice still held its throaty texture. Even though she couldn't reach her former range, it still moved gracefully. Lauren and Shayla provided the back up and by the time they pulled into the driveway, her stomach had settled somewhat and her mind was at ease. There was no need to worry about dinner at the Crawford's. Everything was going to be all right.

Chapter Fifteen

Christmas morning dawned, frosty but clear. Lauren had given up on sleep hours ago and had decided to exercise away her apprehensions. She worked out until her fatigued muscles screamed. Ready for a relaxing bath, she flipped on the lights in her bathroom and twisted the water nozzle.

Cold water trickled into the bathtub and Lauren twisted hot and cold handles, receiving no improved results. No problem, she thought. The water heater was fixed just last week. It's not broken again.

Opening the garage door, she stepped down and didn't immediately register that her sneaker had filled with water. It wasn't until she lowered her other foot, saw jet sprays of water coming from the pipe, did it register.

The pipe was broken!

Lauren felt sick to her stomach. Two hours to get ready for the "Don't be late," doctor and no hot water.

Grabbing the T fashioned key, she lifted the garage door and ran outside to the front lawn to shut off the valve. She twisted the key until it wouldn't turn any more. Her sweaty work out clothes clung to her back like icicles. It was too cold to be outside half dressed and wet.

"No problem." She tried to quell her steadily rising panic. "I'll take a bath the old fashioned way." The days of heating the water in pots on the stove came back. She sloshed inside the garage, squeezing past the side-view mirrors on both cars. She returned the water key to the designated peg on the wall and backed into her shiny car.

The car gleamed from the waxing Eric must have given it. The interior was even scrubbed clean and vacuumed. Must have been during his sleepless night. Her senses whirred at the idea of him thinking of her all night.

Lauren stared at the vertical crack in the pipe. About three inches long one inch wide, it gaped, the final drivel of water leaking out. Anger burned through her. She'd been ripped off. She resisted the urge to kick the heater, and instead planted her foot on a sodden box. To her surprise, out tumbled two silk, dry clean only dresses she had given to Shayla last week to take to the cleaners. Onto the wet ground they plunged, shriveling before her eyes.

"Shayla!" she gasped, staring at the clothes. Residual water from the pipe splashed her hair. "My hair!" Lauren jerked upright, covering her head with her hands. Steaming, she grabbed duct tape off the utility shelf. Reaching up, she tried to cover the hole but couldn't quite get it around, so she planted one foot on the bumper of her car, then established a firm foot hold once she was standing on the hood.

Her hands shook and she steadied herself hoping she could wind it around the rounded surface. She just needed to get a little . . . closer. The tape stuck together on either side of her fingers. Frustrated, Lauren shook her hand. Her sneaker on the shiny wax disagreed and she started to slip.

Lauren fought to stay upright and for the briefest second, thought she had accomplished just that.

Her feet flew from beneath her and she screamed, "No, nooo," before landing against the hood, sliding on her bottom to the bumper of the car.

Shayla opened the garage door and stared at her.

"Ma, did you know there's no hot water?"

Oblivious to Lauren's rising anger, Chaney added, "Have you started the coffee? I just tried the sink, but I got only a trickle."

Lauren rose and tested her legs that were burning from the fall. She rubbed her tender rear end and brushed past them retorting, "Get the pot and scoop some up from the garage floor mother, there's enough out there!"

Lauren stormed up the stairs to her room and slammed the door. Shrugging into her robe, she massaged her sore behind and began hunting for her stockings. Grabbing them off the bed, she hurried to the bathroom and dug under the sink for the blow dryer, while turning on the curlers.

Throwing the stocking on the bathroom counter, she mimicked Eric. "Don't be late. Who does he think he is? I'll be ready." Lauren glanced at the clock. Fooling with the water heater had taken too much time. She had exactly one hour.

"My dress!" She exhaled in panic. The dress she had planned to wear was shriveled to toddler size on the garage floor. Grinding her teeth, Lauren hurried into the closet still rubbing her bottom.

"What's casual?" She asked her clothes, searching for the right outfit. Discarding clothes into a pile, she hopped from one foot to the other.

"Come on perfect outfit," she begged. Ripping cleaners plastic from items, she eyed one two-piece suit in particular. It was a cute, but was it right for meeting your daughter's family for the first time?

"It'll have to do," she decided then smelled something burning. "What in the world . . ."

Rushing back into the bathroom, Lauren stared horrified at

the sight on the counter. In her rush to find the hair dryer under the sink, she had carelessly thrown the stockings on top of the counter. They landed on the curling iron, which melted them into brown goo. The curlers were ruined, and so were her only pair of black hose.

"No, no, no. This is not my life," she moaned, looking at the mess then back at the clock. "Somebody help me." Lauren said quietly and sat down gingerly. "Mama. Shayla," she called.

They both burst into the room and stared at the mess. Chaney crinkled her nose, waving her hand, as she lifted the window. "What are you doing, Lauren? He's going to be here in twenty-five minutes. Why, your hair isn't even done." Tsking, Chaney stared disapprovingly at her daughter. "It's not good to keep a man waiting."

"Mama, he's not a man," she shot back. "I mean he's a man, but . . . It doesn't matter." Lauren put out of her mind just how manly he was and turned to Shayla. "Do you have some stockings I can borrow? I need navy, gray, or black." Shayla nodded quickly.

"Good. Get them. Mama"—her voice now steady, back in control—"put a large pot of water on to boil. Get the distilled water that we use for the iron. It's in the linen closet."

Shayla returned with the stockings while she was in the bathroom and stood anxiously behind her mother blow drying her hair.

"Ma, you shouldn't have worked out today," she offered over the whir of the dryer. "You smell tart." Lauren met her gaze in the mirror.

"Shayla, don't mess with me. It's been a long morning. Go help Grandma with the water."

Rushing into Shayla's bathroom, Lauren picked up her curlers, grateful they were still plugged in. Bumping the ends of her hair, she rolled the curls in small pink curlers and hurried to her tub. There was an inch of water in the tub when Chaney and Shayla finished pouring it in.

They stared at the measly amount and Lauren shrugged. "Oh well, that's going to have to do." She stripped quickly. Lowering herself in the tub, she washed, scooping water in her hands and throwing it over her back. "Shayla, hit my skirt with the iron for me. Mama be on the lookout for . . ." Her eyes gravitated to Shayla's who stood by her bed. "Him." Shayla took the skirt and walked slowly away.

Lauren dried off, powdered and splashed lotion over her body, fast. On the way out the bathroom, she bumped the powder canister and it landed on the floor in a big puff of white clouds. Can't clean it up now. Gotta go. Five to twelve.

Quickly she donned underwear and stockings then searched the bed. "Shayla, my white blouse. Where is it?" Greeted with a mumbled response, Lauren slipped into the lined skirt and stared down at it. It was too short. Too far above the knee. Way too far!

"Ma, that's cute." Shayla handed her the neatly ironed jacket.

"It's too short." Lauren tugged and pulled to no avail. The damn thing would not lengthen.

"No, it's not. Put on the jacket, you don't need a blouse under it." Lauren shrugged into the black and white pin striped jacket and buttoned hurriedly. Shayla yanked rollers from her head, and when Lauren heard her mother's voice, she pushed Shayla toward the door. "I'll finish here. Go talk to . . . Eric." Her hesitation cost her seconds and Lauren ran to the bathroom throwing her towel over the pile of fragrant powder that lay on the floor.

Her makeup went on in record time and she dug on the floor of her closet for her sensible, black mid-heel leather shoes. Her rear still ached and she rubbed it trying to ease the pain.

Finding only black patent leather pumps with extremely high heels, she slipped her feet into them and stabbed her ears with onyx earrings. Checking her appearance in the full length mirror, Lauren shrugged at the length of her skirt and grabbed her tiny handbag. "This is it for today. I can't do any better."

Taking the stairs with hurried steps, she came up behind Eric who stood in the doorway of the den and living room. His broad shoulders blocked her way, and she took a moment to catch her breath, if that were possible, and look at him. Tiny curls of shiny black hair twisted nicely at the base of his scalp and were edged neatly against the collar of a black denim shirt.

When he laughed that deep rich laugh she found hard to resist, his shoulders shrugged and he inserted his hands into the pockets of black denim jeans. She backed up a step as he seemed to turn in slow motion, feeling her presence.

Humorous gray eyes glanced over her and when they returned to her face, masculine appreciation reflected from them. The sexiest grin came to rest on his lips. In an instant, they went from being in a room with others, to being alone. For some reason he nodded and Lauren finally spoke.

"Hello, Doctor Crawford."

He shook his head no. "What's my name?"

Lauren looked away and smiled. "Eric." She walked past him. He grabbed her arm and held her in place, his touch making her want to leap hurdles to get away from him. She prayed she wouldn't have a repeat of her response the last time she saw him.

"Ma, I'm going out to the car with Grandma. Do you have the baby pictures?" Lauren felt for the bag. "I'll get them and be right out." Their daughter walked out leaving them alone.

"I hope you weren't planning to wear this today." Eric pulled a roller from her hair and tossed it on the couch. His fingers worked through the strands of her short hair stroking it into place. Eric rested his large hand on the back of her neck for a moment and Lauren thought she would collapse.

Just being near him set her afire in places where there had been nothing for a very long time. His breath fanned the back of her neck making the hairs stand and bow to him. She stepped forward out of the confines of his hands, and pressed her fingers to the back of her head.

The horn honked and Lauren was pulled from the intense feeling of pleasure the simple gesture caused.

"Wait there's something else," he stepped closer. "Turn around."

"What is it?" Lauren jumped when the first brush fanned across her bottom. The powder! Eric held her away from him and brushed until the last speck of powder was no longer visible on the black and white skirt. Each gentle stroke made her contract her rear, heightening the tension that already flowed down her center. Lauren resisted the urge to lay down right there and give herself to him. His hands felt that good.

"Am I all fixed up now?" she asked shakily. Hoping humor would ease her suffering.

"Yeah, you're fine. Let's go." Eric lifted her coat and held it for her to slide her arms into. Out the door in a flash, he was waiting for her on the passenger side before she caught up with him.

He avoided her eyes and held the door open, peering up the street into the distance. Seconds passed and he exhaled, finally meeting her gaze. His voice rumbled low enough for her ears only. "Get in, Lauren. Before your mother and daughter watch me make love to you on the driveway."

Her heart hammered against her chest so hard she thought it would burst through her skin and land on the paved ground. It all came back in waves. His hands, and his mouth, and his desire all touching her, wanting her. For a moment their eyes met and held and it was all there.

Desire and confusion.

She slid into the car avoiding the knowing glance from her mother and kept her eyes riveted to the blue mat under her feet.

"Is this new?" Shayla asked, once Eric buckled himself in the leather interior of the late model Lincoln Continental.

Eric replied, his head shaking in mock disgust. "It's my father's." He seemed to have recovered Lauren thought, watching him through lowered lids. He lifted his head, staring through the rearview to see. Lauren inhaled and exhaled slowly. She was so close to the brink, she knew if he touched her, she would scream her release all over the front seat of his daddy's car.

It wouldn't be pretty.

Shayla and Chaney talked between themselves and Lauren crossed her right leg over her left. "Eric," Chaney said, "I really loved that little car you had yesterday. You have to promise me we can speed around in it again sometime."

He chuckled at the comment. "Chaney, you set the time, and I'll be there. Lauren?" He stretched his hand out and grazed her skin with his thumb. "Did you know how feisty your mother is?"

Feisty, her mother? "No, I had no idea."

Chaney laughed at his teasing compliment. They rode in silence for a while.

"Ma, Eric has a convertible Mercedes and he said one day he would teach me how to drive it."

"He did." Lauren gave him a sidelong look. He ignored her. She could tell by the way he half smiled, he knew she was looking at him. The talking continued after she closed her eyes.

She listened to the three-way conversation between Eric, her mother, and Shayla. She could tell they hadn't just had lunch when he picked them up from Geoffrey's. Oh, no. They had spent the entire day together. They sounded like one happy group and she fought her mounting jealousy.

Eventually the car slowed and Eric turned up a long gravel drive that wound around tall evergreen trees. When they stopped behind other cars and trucks, the women fell silent looking up at the imposing mansion. Lauren heard Shayla catch her breath.

Unfastening his seat belt, he turned to them. Two pairs of hazel eyes stared at him, and another set, identical to his own, stared back.

"There's nothing to be nervous about," he reassured. "This is my family, which is your family now, and they're all excited to meet you. They're really nice people," he said and grabbed Lauren's hand on the seat loosening her grip on Shayla's baby photos. The heat of his large hand eased some of the chill from her stiff fingers.

He looked directly at Shayla and reached over the seat to give her hands a squeeze. "It's going to be all right. Anytime you need something, you look for me, and I'll be there."

Shayla nodded and closed her eyes before opening the car door. They all followed suit and soon were standing side by side on the sidewalk. Eric took Shayla's hand and held tight before climbing the stairs to the big house.

Lauren followed her mom, who used her arm when she needed support.

Eric turned to check their progress after he and Shayla reached the top. Lauren felt as if she were in a scene from a horror movie the way the door creeped open and thirty pairs of gray eyes stared at them.

There were Crawfords everywhere as the door closed behind them and Lauren stared into the eyes of her daughter.

Shayla was a Crawford.

Chapter Sixteen

"I'm Vivian Crawford. Welcome to our home." The matriarch of the family stepped forward and warmly greeted Lauren and Chaney with a kiss on the cheek and a big hug. Gray streaked her hair and it was caught in a tidy bun at the back of her head. Her eyes were warm and curious as she came to stand before Shayla.

She waited for the young girl to make eye contact with her before she spoke in a clear voice laced with love. "Welcome home, Granddaughter."

She pulled Shayla to her and hugged her tight, rocking her in her arms. Lauren felt her protective barrier begin to slip and tried to swallow the lump in her throat. One by one, tall Crawford men, their children, and wives were introduced to them.

The place erupted in loud chatter as Lauren, Shayla, and Chaney took off their coats. Kids ran around as they were ushered into the family room. Lauren gaped at the sight of the ten-foot fir tree that dominated the living room. She only glanced in the room as she passed because it was impossible to enter. The amount of wrapped packages nearly overflowed the room.

Everything twinkled and bells rang, while Nat King Cole music played in the background. The house smelled delicious and Lauren walked around still a bit nervous following Eric and Shayla.

"Do you want something to drink?" Eric asked after Shayla peeled herself from his side and went downstairs to the basement with the other teenagers.

"Yes, thank you," she said and smiled, looking for her mother as she tugged self-consciously at her skirt.

"I'll be right back." He disappeared through a door at the end of the room. As soon as he left her side, four tall Crawford men surrounded her.

"I'm Julian," the tallest man said. He offered her a seat on the sofa, then sat beside her. Lauren still had to lean back and look up to see his face.

"I'm Michael," the other said. "This is Edwin, and Justin." Lauren forced a friendly smile to her face. They eyed her speculatively for a few moments.

"Am I on trial?" she asked, aiming her question at Julian and Michael.

"No," they answered in unison, caught off guard.

Lauren ran her hands down her thighs and folded them in her lap. "Then let's talk about Eric and Shayla. That is why you all surrounded me, right?"

"What do you want from Eric?" Julian asked, his manner guarded and professional. He wasn't as handsome as the other Crawford men, because of the less than friendly glint in his gray eyes.

"I want one million dollars, a new car, and a fur coat." The collective stares were surprised. All except Julian's.

"I knew it!" he exclaimed, satisfaction lacing his voice.

"From you." Now that she had his attention, Lauren leaned forward meeting each of their captivated gazes.

"Let me tell you something. I don't want anything from Eric, personally. For my daughter, I want him to keep his promises to her, treat her nicely when they're together, and show up when he says he will. I want *them* to establish a relationship they will be comfortable with and I'm going to do everything in my power to help that happen."

"There's got to be more." Julian insisted watching her closely. He simply couldn't believe she would only want Eric to bear the full responsibility of his acceptance of Shayla as his daughter.

"What would you like me to do? Ask for money, beg for repayment?"

"I knew we would get around to the nuts and bolts of it. Lady, you're not going to get a dime . . ."

"I don't know how to say this other than to be straight forward. I considered suing to keep Eric away from Shayla. I was advised by my attorney Clarissa Chambers that he would have recourse against me if he could prove paternity. Your brother would have gone to any end to know that Shayla was his. Now that it's been proven, I still don't want anything from him except," she emphasized looking right at Julian, "what he promises to my daughter."

Lauren pointed a finger at each of them. "If I were you, I would wonder if he can live up to his responsibility, and not be so concerned with what *my* motivation is."

"But—"

"Leave her alone," Michael demanded with stiff authority. His assistance eased the panic she felt rising within her. As calm as she pretended to be on the outside, the pressure of them combined was enough to unravel any unsuspecting soul. Lauren met each of their gazes evenly.

"I've prepared for my daughter's future. The finances for her education are already in place. I've saved for her wedding. She's *my* daughter." Her voice thickened with resolve. "I will never take money from Eric. Now if this little getting-to-know-you session is over, I'd like to get something to drink. Or is that suspicious behavior, too?''

Lauren waited for long legs to draw back as she stood. ''Excuse me.'' The last pair of legs belonging to Julian eased out of her way.

She looked back after she was a safe distance away and couldn't believe she saw respect mirrored in their eyes. They were tough and protective. All the things she expected in a family. She even got a thumbs up from Michael. Well, I've won one over, she thought and gave him a thankful smile.

Eric stood at the table with his back to her. She couldn't explain it, but the attraction was outside of anything she had ever experienced before. They didn't have a long relationship to draw from. They hadn't known each other for years and years. It was something deeper, more physical, more natural. He seemed to know and so did she. Yet she couldn't explain it. There weren't any words. It just was. And that was the hardest thing to accept. It was so foreign. Therefore something to be afraid of.

Although Eric continued in his discussion, he wrapped his arm loosely around her waist and held her. The gesture was far from casual and Lauren couldn't stop the burn that rose from the small of her back all the way to her cheeks. She looked up at the handsome man and tried to gauge whether he'd had any sleep as he promised he wouldn't. She certainly hadn't.

Lauren gravitated closer to him, remembering what happened on her front step, for her entire neighborhood to see, had they been awake. She felt the pressure rising again and moved away from his thumb which idly stroked her ribs. Eric continued the slow torture, oblivious to the sensations now shooting up from her feet. If she moved again, he would glaze the side of her breast! Lauren accepted his teasing strokes, her nose beginning to sweat from the reaction to his touch.

If she did what she wanted, which was to lay back and moan

loudly, Julian would surely have grounds to haul her into court on public indecency charges.

She cleared her throat and tried to escape from the confines of Eric's arm, but he gently restricted her movement, with the splayed pressure of his fingers on her back.

"Pop, it's not like that."

"Do the right thing." The elder man took her hand.

"Pop," Eric implored, but his father dragged Lauren with him. Lauren looked longingly back at him and went along with the big man.

"Everybody calls me Pop, because I'm the daddy of these children." He gestured dismissively toward the couch full of grown men. "All my grandchildren call me Poppa." Lauren nodded as he walked her to the furthest corner of the room to look at a wall of pictures. "These are my children when they were babies.

Julian and Michael are sixteen months apart. Justin, Edwin, and Nick are all eleven months apart. Eric followed two years later." He looked at her teasingly. "He's the runt."

Lauren relaxed. This man was very powerful, despite what Eric said about his mother being the head of this family. Pop Crawford was in complete control.

Instantly she liked him. He gave her the history of each son, their children, and wives until names jumbled together in her head. He stopped at the picture of Nick and stared at his picture.

"Did Eric tell you about Nick?"

"No sir," she answered quietly. Lauren remembered he mentioned him once, but seemed pained by the memory.

"Call me Pop, young lady." It was an order, and Lauren intended to follow it. "He will when he's ready." Lauren was treated to a complete tour of the house finding its grandeur outstanding.

Unexpectedly, Pop held her upper arms and said, "If my son had any sense in his head, he would let me marry you two today."

Lauren held her flaming cheeks, her face registering the surprise that reverberated through her body. By then, Eric was at her side. His father released her and joined their hands.

"Very nice, son." Pop smiled approvingly at them. "Now do something about it." With the authority his position commanded, Pop Crawford clasped his hands behind his back and walked off, joining his other sons in their heated discussion about politics.

"He's something else isn't he?" Eric turned and raked his gaze over her face. It rested between her chin and chest.

Lauren consciously practiced breathing. "He's definitely something."

"I like . . . your pearls." Her vision blurred, she stared at his lips so long. She slid her eyes to his which were preoccupied watching her. "You don't take compliments too well, do you?"

"Y-Yes. Of course."

"Where's you jade necklace?"

"I traded it in today for these pearls. Do you like them?"

"I said I did about five minutes ago, when you were daydreaming. I hope it was about me."

"No," she lied, but then added, "Thank you."

Eric's eyes twinkled and she took a sip from the glass he held to her lips. Déjà vu.

"Maybe I'll go help in the kitchen," she said, afraid that standing there for too long with him would make her do something foolish.

"Oh, no, you won't." Eric hand was still clasped hers and he pulled her to a large sitting area in the corner of the room Pretty women sat there. The Crawford women.

"This is April, Keisha, and Ann. Meet the women who run my life."

Eric left her standing among curious stares.

Chapter Seventeen

Lauren wiped tears from her eyes as Ann, Edwin's wife, ended a hilarious story about the Crawford brothers and their Thursday night pro basketball games in the yard.

The women took her by surprise, and welcomed her into their close circle. There wasn't a hint of jealousy or competition among them. They were an enviable group. All beautiful, but comfortable with each other.

Several times she glanced up and found Eric watching her. The hungry look in his eyes was enough to coax out the flirt in her. Lauren enjoyed the delicious feeling as she casually rocked her leg, watching him lick his lips. Ordinarily, she wouldn't have flirted. She didn't do it often enough to be good at it. But the look in his eye wasn't ordinary. Not by any means. She knew it was a dangerous game, but she couldn't resist playing.

Eric stalked around the table, ignoring the conversation his brother's were having, nursing his drink. Lauren recrossed her legs and laughed, her eyes full of merriment when he missed his mouth and poured some punch down his shirt front. He wiped the moisture away and gave her a sardonic look that promised to get her back.

She turned her attention back to the conversation between April, Michael's wife, and Keisha, Julian's better half.

"Work it girl." Ann playfully nudged her arm.

"I beg your pardon?" Lauren tried to look innocent, but couldn't keep a straight face.

"It's about time for Eric to get serious."

"Oh, we're not serious. In fact we're nothing."

"Really?" Keisha replied sweetly. "Well if you cross your legs one more time, something else besides Eric's shirt will be wet." The three sisters-in-law broke into gales of laughter and Lauren blushed, embarrassed.

"Is it that obvious?"

Ann smiled and patted her arm. "Crawford men are very hard to resist. Look at them. They're beautiful."

As if on cue Edwin turned to his wife and winked. Her voice was shuddery when she spoke. "They all work hard. They come from a good family and Edwin is so good to me."

"Do you have children?"

"Six," Ann replied.

Lauren couldn't keep her eyes from widening in surprise. "My goodness, you've been blessed. You have your hands full." April stood and hurried away. "Did I say something?"

Keisha stood too. Six feet tall in bare feet, Lauren watched the statuesque woman glide toward her brother-in-law. She returned after a moment and seated herself on the other side of Lauren. "She's a little sensitive. Michael's going to see about her. They've been trying to have a baby for several years. So far nothing."

"I'm sorry. I know this whole thing with Shayla has probably thrown the entire family for a loop."

The women leaned forward, forming a tight circle. Keisha, the ringleader spoke. "You're welcome here. Eric is a changed man since you and Shayla came into his life and it's for the better. We all worried about him and his ways. But he's a changed man. But no matter what happens between you and him, your daughter will always be loved.''

''Thank you.'' A great weight lifted off her shoulders. ''Shouldn't we help in the kitchen?''

The women leaned back and crossed their legs in one practiced motion. ''Lauren, this is Christmas,'' April said. ''If you try to help Ma Viv in her kitchen, she might slice something off of you. You'll see when it's your turn.''

''My turn?''

Ann shushed Keisha who started to laugh. ''We might scare her off if you tell her about the holidays.''

Quizzically she stared at them. ''You're not leaving until I know what you're talking about.''

''You really want to know?'' Ann asked.

Lauren nodded. Keisha sat forward. ''We celebrate every holiday. From New Years at the beginning of the year to Kwanzaa at the end. And we rotate houses so no one does all the cooking.''

''There are at least seven holidays that I can think of off the top of my head,'' amazed Lauren stared at them. ''You're joking.''

Keisha's face was full of merriment. ''Oh, no honey. I think we're up to about twenty-two, now. Then we come over for Thursday night basketball. We even celebrate Groundhog Day and the first day of summer.''

Lauren laughed, totally relaxed for the first time in a long time.

The wail of children stopped their giggles and Keisha and Ann picked up their respective little ones.

''Uncle Eric,'' the little boy named Aaron wailed, holding out his hand. Eric crossed the room in two strides and took the crying child from Keisha's arms.

''I-hurt-my-hannnd.''

Lauren leaned forward to see the injury as a silky feeling flooded her as she watched Eric handle the child.

"Hey, buddy, what happened? Let me take a look."

The little boy unfolded his fingers and showed Eric his palm. One long sliver of wood was wedged underneath the skin. The splinter looked painful even to her eyes and Lauren watched Eric as he adroitly shifted the boy to his side and walked him to the hall bathroom. Keisha took her hand and pulled her along behind her and they stood in the door.

"You know what, I can get this out real easy but you have to be brave. Okay, Kyle? Are you a warrior?"

Sniffles precluded Kyle from nodding his head, but under Eric's confident smile he finally gave in.

"All right then, sit here on my lap. We have to wash it first then I'm going to take this thing out. We'll give it to Mom later and have her put it in your scrap book." He hugged him tight then gently washed his hand. Keisha handed him the tweezers and he talked in a normal voice as he eased the wood from his hand.

"All done." Despite Eric's speech about being a warrior, little Kyle buried his face in his uncle's shirt and cried. Lauren would have expected Eric to give him a speech about boys not crying and being tough, but he just cradled him in his arms and soothed him until his tears ceased. A lump rose in her throat as she watched the tender moment between man and child and something pulled at her heart strings.

Keisha took the child and Eric washed and dried his hands. Lauren felt her eyes well when he leaned over and kissed the little boy's head before leaving the bathroom. He draped his arm over her shoulder and turned her away from the den.

"You were very good with him." Lauren followed his lead up the stairs.

"I love these kids. Up until a month ago, they were all I had. I love having a daughter of my very own. Maybe one day—" he drifted off and opened the door to a room.

"One day what?" she asked walking inside. She focused on the outdated wallpaper, then the two twin beds. She realized she was in Eric's boyhood room and turned to him.

"Maybe one day I'll be able to give Shayla brothers and sisters." Lauren backed away from him, coughing to cover her shock. Eric and babies of his own?

She focused on a series of photos on the wall and recognized a picture of him. He was smiling broadly.

"When was this taken?" she asked, diverting the subject to something safe.

"When I graduated from medical school. My mom calls this her wall of fame. Pictured here are all the Crawford men. She wants her grandchildren to have role models to look up to so she had these pictures made of each one of us and hung. When the kids come over they sleep in this room. They have men to look up to."

"That's a wonderful idea."

She spotted one picture of a man who looked almost identical to him. "Who's he, Eric? Is this Nick?"

"Come on, let's go." Eric grabbed her hand and she stumbled into him. His arms automatically went around her and they both froze. His touch was hesitant at first but as she stayed close, he eventually enveloped her.

"We don't have to talk about it," she whispered. "But if I recall correctly, you helped me through something very tough. I thought I might return the favor."

"His plane crashed, killing my wife."

Lauren reached up and caressed his cheek. "I'm so sorry."

He urged her cheek against his chest. "It wasn't his fault, but after he was cleared by the FAA, he disappeared. The family occasionally gets a postcard, but nobody has seen him. It's been almost two years." Eric's fingers stroked her head and held her close. Lauren heard the steady thump of his heart and wrapped her arms around his waist. She couldn't help it. She *wanted* to comfort him. His height made such a difference in how they stood. He had to lean down just to fully hold her against him. But she loved it. She loved being wrapped in his arms. She hadn't realized until just then how much she'd looked forward to today.

"Maybe one day he'll come home and you two can talk."

"I hope so," he said, although his voice echoed hallowly. He turned the knob on the door, but kept it closed. He seemed about to say something.

The dinner bell rang and Eric drew her away. A stampede sounded from both levels of the house. Little Crawford's and big surrounded the tables that stretched wide and long, full of food.

Lauren caught a glimpse of her mother who smiled, beguiled by a new friend, Roscoe Burnside. Everyone stood silently around the table and linked hands, as Pop Crawford said the prayer thanking God for the food and the hands that prepared it.

Everyone chorused "amen" and they all made lots of noise sitting down, passing bowls and plates, and eating. Eric sat between her and Shayla filling their plates with food.

He and Shayla kept up a running conversation until Shayla started to tell him about their morning. Lauren shook her head, and shot Shayla a warning glance. Soon the entire table was involved in the discussion and everyone laughed hysterically when Chaney piped in how her controlled daughter lost it when she torched her stockings on the curlers. Lauren laughed, too. Looking back, it was funny.

"Why didn't you call me?" Eric asked, his hand inching higher on her thigh. He knew what he was doing, the pervert. Her thighs began to quiver yet his expression remained devilishly innocent. Lauren's fork clattered against her plate, then fell to the floor.

"Sorry," she said embarrassed. Eric reached down and picked it up. He walked to the kitchen and brought her a clean fork.

"I didn't need any help. It was quite simple. All I had to do was turn the water off." she said, in defense of her actions. "Tomorrow I'll call the repairman and he'll come out and fix it again." She held up her hands in surrender. "It's handled. Thank you very much."

"I'll be there when he gets there. You probably got ripped off."

"No I didn't." Lauren wanted to wipe that self-deprecating I-know-more-than-you smile off his charming face although that had been her conclusion too. "I thoroughly checked this guy out. He was very highly recommended."

Unfazed by her defensiveness, Eric asked, "By who?"

"His brother."

Eric's brothers burst out laughing. Mashed potatoes and gravy stuck to the roof of her mouth and Lauren tried to swallow the gooey lump. She completed her meal in silence. The teenagers quickly vacated the table followed by the small children, leaving the Crawford men and their women at the table alone.

Lauren picked at her dessert and Eric leaned over whispering in her ear.

"You're not angry are you? We weren't laughing at you. We were laughing at the situation."

"No, I'm not angry. It's just—"

"What?" he whispered as if they were sharing intimate secrets. And the way his arm hung loosely across the back of her chair was unnerving, also.

"I like nothing better than being the joke of dinner."

Lauren met his look levelly and felt herself getting lost in the power of his gaze. His eyes exuded such a strong magnetism. The more often she was in his presence, the closer in she was drawn.

She sucked the sweet potato pie off the end of her fork and sat back in the chair crossing her legs, full and comfortable.

"You're too serious. Nobody is making you the joke of

anything.'' Perhaps he was right. The day had turned out well. Eric sat back in his chair. ''What are you thinking about now?''

His fingers gently stroked the bend under her knee sending electric currents through her. The pleasant scrutiny of his gaze made her want to conjure up images of him with fangs, or a horn nose. But her imagination failed her. All she saw was a wonderful son, capable doctor and loving father to her daughter. The view wasn't bad at all.

''That I should thank you for making today special for Shayla.'' She surprised him by kissing his cheek. Eric turned his head and she received the full pleasure of his lips against hers.

The palms of her hands itched to roam over his skin. Twitterings of longing shot from her toes, through the back of her legs, snaked up her spine, and ended with a thump in her chest. She went dizzy with desire. He tugged at her bottom lip, then broke away.

''Come on,'' he gestured to his family who beamed at them. ''Let's open these presents so we can go.'' Eric reached down and took Lauren's hand assisting her from the table.

Chapter Eighteen

Ten pairs of jeans lay in Shayla's pile of presents and there was still more. Lauren shook her head at the huge amount of gifts his family showered on her. *Where are we going to put all this?*

Eric handed Shayla a slim, embossed envelop with a kiss and Shayla looked at it curiously. Her shocked gasp gave way to tears and Lauren stood up, confused as Shayla hugged him crying.

"Shayla, what is it?" she asked, her head pounding, dread creeping through her.

"Emory! He gave me Emory." Shayla held up the envelope and read, her voice quivering with emotion.

"Dear Shayla: I missed seventeen birthdays, and as many Christmases. Your first steps and newest teeth are something I can never recapture. But I can give you the future you dreamed of. Here is your ticket to the world. What you make of it is up to you, go with the best of intentions and succeed." She then held up the paper.

"He gave me a eighteen thousand dollar certificate of deposit for Emory." Collective gasps went up and no one spoke.

Lauren took the outstretched envelop from her daughter's hand and stared at it. Sure enough, it was a certificate of deposit that matured in six months. Helpless anger rose within her and she sputtered ready to give it back, but was halted by her daughters enthusiasm.

"Ma, isn't this great? I can't believe it. I'm going to the school of my dreams." Shayla hopped happily from one foot to another and kissed her father, taking the certificate from her mother's slack hand showing it to her grandparents and uncles.

The tension in the room was palpable and lessened several degrees by the impatience of the youngest children. Dismissed, with their older brother and sisters the group of kids left the grown-ups alone. "Eric," Edwin said. "Sometimes, you're just stupid. Lauren, I hope you don't think his blindness is in all of us." He turned to the family. "Let's give them some privacy."

Lauren looked at Eric and resisted the impulse to scratch his eyes out. "You could have warned me," she muttered keeping her voice low.

"I don't care what my family thinks. I don't have to ask your permission to give my daughter a gift." Defiantly, his gray eyes flashed. In some ways Eric was worse than Hank. Eric used snake oil charm.

"You made me look like a fool in front of my daughter and your family." Lauren couldn't mask the hurt that seeped into her voice. "You knew I could never give her that. You should have told me first." She started to say something else but dropped her hand and pressed her trembling lips together. "I'm ready to go now."

The beautiful day was over. The warmth of his family's generosity was gone leaving her with a terrible feeling of isolation and loneliness. He'd made a fool of her. He made her exactly what Julian already suspected. A money-grubbing opportunist.

"Ma, is everything okay?"

Lauren looked into her daughter's eyes, then over her head meeting Eric's. "Your father and I are having a disagreement about something."

"You're not going to make me give back the money are you?" Shayla's voice trembled and her eyes filled. Lauren was trapped. Caught in Eric's web.

Lauren patted her arm. "No," she whispered. "Go say good-bye to everyone. It's time to go."

Shayla looked between her parents then walked away, her head down. Lauren turned away from Eric's piercing gaze and began loading the presents into bags.

"Let me help."

She shoved his hand away, standing tall. "The kind of help you give is exactly what I don't need." Her shoulders brushed his arm as he threw up his hands in frustration and walked a short distance away. Anger smoldered in the depths of his eyes and stiffened his shoulders. She grabbed a white plastic gift bag and stuffed jeans in without folding them.

She had to get out of there. He had undermined her in front of Shayla. Deflated her moment to shine in Shayla's eyes. *I had plans.* She wanted to brain scream selfishly.

". . . I always, always wanted Emory. Do you think it's too late? Do you think I'll get in?"

Lauren jerked up her head. Shayla stood with her new grand-father in the grand foyer in the grand house. It's grandeur nauseated her. Shayla's beaming smile spoke as a testament to her feelings. *I've lost her.*

Lauren released the remainder of her dissipating anger with a heavy sigh and tied the bag, reaching for another.

"I can show you how to hurt a man and leave no scars," Keisha, Julian's wife offered. Lauren recalled she said she was a black belt in karate. Keisha held the bag for her.

"I may need your advice later." The two women hugged before being surrounded by all the Crawford women. The lines were drawn and Eric clearly was the loser of this dispute.

"Lauren," her mother cut in, breaking up the group. Sliding into her wool coat. "Roscoe has asked me to come over and have an after-dinner drink. He'll bring me home."

Chaney slid her arms into her coat sleeves. Lauren pulled her mother off to the side. Had everybody lost their minds? "Mom, are you sure? You just met this man."

"Well, honey, how will I get to know him way over at your place?" Chaney patted her hand and winked. "You're so protective. How do you think you got here?" The shock must have registered on her face because Chaney laughed and so did Roscoe when he helped Chaney with her scarf.

He stepped away from her mother. He grasped Lauren's hand meeting her gaze with a friendly smile.

"Lauren, I'm not in the habit of compromising beautiful women. We're just going to the laser show at Stone Mountain, then to my house for a quick night cap. Do we have your permission?"

Embarrassed, Lauren turned her hand in his and shook. "Of course. Have a good time."

She waited with bags in hand in the high-ceilinged foyer for Eric who was in a hot discussion with his mother.

Vivian walked over and hugged her.

"Goodbye, Lauren. You're welcome here anytime. Chaney, you too. Goodnight, Roscoe." The two grandmothers hugged a long time. When they pulled away, tears glistened in both their eyes.

"We had a wonderful time. Happy New Year," Lauren said, returning Vivian's embrace. It smothered her remaining anger. She walked to the car. Eric and his brother's loaded the bags into the trunk.

He slid into the car slapping his hands together against the winter air, and Lauren ignored him, turning to Shayla who rested her head against the back seat.

"Shayla did you have a good—" A light tapping on the window made her turn and Lauren depressed the button rolling it down. Renee, Shayla's cousin stood outside. She and Shayla favored so much it was startling.

"Can Shayla stay for a while? My mom said we could go to the movies and we wanted her to go, too." Shayla sat up immediately. The desolate expression she wore was gone.

"Plee-aase, Ma. Can I?"

Lauren hesitated a moment then gave in. "Okay. Are you sure it's okay with your mother to bring Shayla home? We live kind of far."

Shayla had already gotten out of the car and was grinning from ear to ear jumping up and down with her cousin. Their laughter was contagious and Lauren laughed too.

"It's no problem, is it, Uncle Eric?"

"No, baby it isn't. If it's too late, call okay?"

"Okay," the two chorused.

"Ma, can I have some money? I'm kind of broke."

Shayla's dimples were prominent when her father peeled off two twenties and handed them to her. Lauren crumpled the ten dollar bill she had been about to hand Shayla and dropped it inside her pocket.

A knot grew tighter in her stomach then burst when Shayla impetuously ran around the car and kissed Eric on the cheek. Lauren watched her run up the stairs of the house and was rewarded with a careless wave before Shayla disappeared inside.

The ride home was quiet. The silence dragged on until she couldn't take it anymore.

"How could you?" She hated herself for hurting so bad.

"Give our daughter eighteen thousand dollars?" he said, completing her sentence. "Because I want her to have the best. I know you've invested more in her than me. And I know it was underhanded and selfish. But face it, Lauren, you're a hard act to follow.''

"Oh, no,'' she said, sarcastically. ''Don't blame me for what happened in your life. You intentionally didn't tell me you were going to give her that money. I already told you I had everything planned. Her education is already taken care of. I already had the money.''

"Do you hear yourself,'' he demanded, the car hurtling up the highway. ''Nobody could pierce that perfectly planned existence of Lauren Michaels.''

"Slow down!''

"Why? You don't ever speed?'' Eric held the car at the high pace then slowed. ''I won't apologize for giving her the money. I want her to have it.''

Lauren crossed her arms over her chest and looked out the passenger window.

"What about Shayla?'' he asked. ''She really wants to go to Emory.''

"You don't always get what you want.'' *I've been explaining that to her for years.* ''Life isn't always fair. But she is getting a good education at the college we chose for her.''

"Think of what *she* wants. She really wants to go to Emory.''

"I know she wants to go there.'' Helplessly she threw her hands into the air. ''It was already settled. Mercer is a fine university. She would have been just as happy there.'' *It was the best I could do.* They covered the remaining twenty miles in silence.

Eric pulled into her driveway and cut off the engine. A cold easterly wind shook the car and Lauren sat quietly, her fight gone.

"I wanted her to go there, too, Eric. I just couldn't afford it. You gave her forty dollars tonight, and I was going to give her ten.'' She turned her face to the window and drew her hand from her pocket the money crumpled in her palm.

He cursed lowly and straightened her hand. "I didn't mean to hurt you," he said softly, trying to draw her close.

"You're giving her unrealistic expectations," she said quietly. "When I first brought her home, she thought I would change my mind and let LeShay take her back. She slept with me for almost a year after Hank died afraid if we weren't together, I would leave. I don't want you ruining what I've tried to build for the past twelve years."

"I'm new at this." He stroked the back of her hair. "I'm going to make mistakes. Do stupid things, like give her eighteen thousand dollars without talking to you first." He caressed her cheek, coaxing a small smile from her. "Should I be punished because I want the best for her? I don't want to disappoint her."

Lauren stared out the front window at the pale garage. The wind howled, shaking the car again and she huddled deeper in her coat.

"No, I don't either," she finally said, looking at him. "Talk to me first. We can come to some agreement. Okay?"

He nodded, moving closer, his hand tightening on the back of her neck. The kiss was imminent, but she backed away at the last second. She fumbled in her purse for her keys afraid to be alone with him on this cold night any longer. She wasn't angry anymore, just hungry, for something she hadn't had in a long time.

When he took them from her hand, she didn't protest.

Eric carried in the two full plastic bags of gifts, stopped and turned on the living room light.

"I'll take these up."

"Top center," Lauren said, closing the door against the wind.

He dragged the bags up the stairs. She suddenly had an image of herself kissing Santa Claus. Eric was perfect, as snow flakes salted his mustache and beard. Lauren kicked off her shoes and hurried to the kitchen.

He's got to go. Leave, she pleaded leaning against the wall, her eyes closed, the heavy coat falling off her left shoulder. He was near. She could smell his intoxicating cologne.

Lauren opened her eyes to find him watching her.

"Can I get you something to drink before you go?"

"I'm not going anywhere." The words curled seductively out of his mouth. He walked toward her.

"You're . . . you're, going home."

He shook his head, as his gaze stalked her with black panther determination. "I'd like some ice water."

"Okay," she whispered, her throat void of moisture. Her hands shook as she pulled down a glass. She filled it with ice and water and handed it to him, careful that their hands didn't touch.

Curiously, she watched him drain the water in long gulps and grew strangely warm when he took one cube in his mouth. Taking her hand, he led her from the kitchen to the moon-lit living room. He sat down on the couch and pulled her until she stood before him.

His fingers flicked out and her coat slipped from her shoulders and fell, gathering at her stocking feet. Her body came alive when he touched her collarbone and drew a line down to the center of her breasts. Lauren closed her eyes, the intensity of naked desire blasting from his eyes making her yearn to be fulfilled.

His long fingers released the button from the hole, then the second one and traced an invisible line to the top button of her jacket. Parting it at the waist, his fingers splayed against her waist and eased the pinstriped jacket down.

Lauren raised her hands to his clothed chest, circling his neck when he drew her closer, her breasts even with his mouth. She exhaled when his cold tongue landed against the hot flesh of her breastbone.

A tiny sliver of the remaining ice slid between her breasts and melted.

Lauren panted reaching behind herself and unhooked her bra. She watched her breasts respond to him as he pulled from the front and freed the pimpled tips.

She kneeled on the couch, sucking air through clenched teeth as he sucked her hot flesh into his cool mouth. His tongue was a conductor for her heat, bringing her flesh to fiery heights as he licked the nipple and captured it with his teeth.

"The light is on," she whispered, her breath coming in short fasts bursts.

"I want to see you," he growled, curving her body into his mouth so he could better claim her.

"Somebody will see."

Eric had begun to unzip her short skirt, and stopped long enough to turn off the light. Cast into silhouette, Lauren slid down closer to him.

"No. Stand." She did as he said and waited while he reached around her to the table.

When his lips touched her again they were ice cold. This time she couldn't resist calling out his name in a near scream. "What are you doing to me?" Lauren's legs wobbled as he reached beneath her skirt and tugged at her panty hose.

"I hate these things. Don't wear them again."

Lauren nodded. Anything. She would have agreed to anything just to have his mouth on her again. His tongue worked magic on her skin, until she was near tears with longing. Every part of her was sensitive to him. His hands and mouth made her cry out. It felt so good. He ripped the hose, dragging her panties with them. Her skirt remained and he gathered it around her waist. He reached for the glass again and in anticipation of the deliciously torturous pleasure he was about to give her she fell against him.

Eric laid her flat on the couch and slid to his knees onto the floor. He dragged the ice cube from her ankle to the inside of her thigh and she quivered at the erotic sensations. He was in complete control and she stretched her hand out grabbing his shoulders, urging him to end the torture with one . . . long . . . stroke of his tongue.

She nearly bolted off the couch when cold ice met her heated desire. It melted, but she widened and exploded when his lips covered her tiny erection.

The combination was like spontaneous combustion.

Lauren arched toward him, all conscious thought escaping her. Her peak was fast approaching and he slid his finger in and out then replaced it with his tongue. He thrust into her, the first contraction quivering. Lauren screamed and soared into the wonderful black abyss of pleasure.

Chapter Nineteen

Although her explosive spiral wasn't complete, Eric swooped her into his arms and carried her up the stairs. She buried her face in his neck, the remaining rockets of desire shooting through her leaving her weak and breathless.

"No more ice." She sighed raggedly when he set the glass on the night table.

Eric nipped at her breast then said with a sly smile, "I can't promise." He brushed everything off the bed and laid her in the center. Within moments he was naked.

Lauren squirmed on the cool sheets, her body hot and ready. She watched as he dug into the pocket of his pants and laid the contents on the nightstand. Several blue foil packets contrasted with the gold of his money clip and green bills.

"Better to be safe than sorry." He pulled her up to him. Once again his voice exuded sensuality transferring the dull warm ache in her center to laser heat. His eyes made promises that his hands and mouth delivered. Every inch of her body awakened to his caresses. Lauren couldn't stay still as she blossomed under his touch. Her inexperience didn't seem to matter to him. She cast her doubts aside and closed her eyes leaning against him as his desire stood up between them. He embraced her and fondled the smooth caramel skin down her back, over her buttocks to the back of her thighs where he parted her and stroked.

Lauren stretched on the bed reaching for him. He joined her as they lay side-by-side, and guided her hand down closing it around himself. She felt pure feminine power when he groaned in pleasure from the long strokes. He claimed her mouth finally, pressing her breast into his broad chest as she bunched her hands between them. "You have hair." she exhaled, surprised.

"I'm aware of that." She shuddered when he took each finger into his mouth and sucked.

"In the calendar, there was nothing there."

He rolled her to her back, kissing her lips. "They . . . shaved . . . it." His fingers tickled the neatly trimmed hair and he stroked her center, sliding his finger in the moist heat, eventually replacing it with his tongue again.

He moved up, not wanting her to go without him again.

Lauren bit the inside of her cheeks and had a knee jerk reaction to his erotic, plunging tongue by snapping her thighs closed around his neck. He growled his approval when she screamed her orgasm.

Her sweat slick body, and pulsating walls broke his control. Eric lifted her knees as he moved above her. He swore in appropriate expletives when she grasped his organ and guided it into her depths. The moist space was home and he made himself comfortable. He couldn't thrust into her just yet. It would have been over within seconds. He had to stop thinking, too, about how wet she was and how ready her body was to please him. If he kept thinking . . .

"Eric."

"Mmm. Hold on baby," he groaned when she moved beneath him. She wrapped her arms around his neck and he rested on his forearms closing her body in. She was so small. Everything about her was petite and he didn't want to hurt her. He withdrew, then slid in real slow. But beneath him, Lauren had her own ideas. She wrapped her arms around his back and grabbed his behind roughly. The thrust she put on him was hard.

Her mouth was demanding and when she took her lips from his, their breath mingled in short puffs as he pushed into her, one hard thrust after another.

From then on there were no misunderstandings about how Lauren liked to be made love to. Eric obliged, his fears dissipated about hurting her. Her body was fully accommodating. He waited until he heard the familiar whimper that led to her complete release and pushed one final time straining to hold on, unwilling to let go. Finally he shot, cast into the sensual super tidal wave of Lauren.

Eric lay awake watching Lauren sleep. He wondered if she knew how loud she snored. It wasn't that she made gross, snorting noises. No, that was too indelicate for his lady love. She purred.

The dip between her shoulder and chin rose and fell with her even breathing as she lay flat on her back her arm wide across the bed. She wore abandon well. Just seeing her bare for him, made the yearning stir within him again.

He couldn't say when he had fallen in love with her. But laying here with her in her frilly, cream-colored room, the floor strewn with clothes, felt right.

She turned onto her stomach, her leg pulling the sheet with her. He let it go, just so he could watch her erotic show. The smooth skin down her back was the perfect color of caramel. Her bottom was perfect. Face it, he thought, smiling, she had a great butt. He guided his hand over it, loving the sound of her purr as she turned beneath his palm. He would wake her up and give it to her again. If she liked the ice . . .

Three crisp beeps interrupted his perusal and he lunged for

the rectangular box that hung from the waist on his pants. Reading the numbers, he peeked at Lauren then raised the phone off the hook and dialed.

"Hey, Ann. It's me, Eric. You're on your way? Okay. Did Shayla have a good time?" He laughed and leaned against the headboard. The covers moved and Lauren curved her body around his. He moved the receiver from his mouth gently kissing her lips, his nature rising. Lauren was a natural aphrodisiac. "All right," he kept his hand on the curve of her hip, the conversation already boring him. He had other business he had to attend to. "I'll try to be gone before you get here. Later."

Lauren laid her hand on his thigh and he never felt such an overpowering passion. The cradle for the phone seemed far away and he dropped it near the base. Her mouth beckoned and he answered, funneling all his love into that one kiss.

"I've got to go. They're on their way."

"I understand." Lauren broke the suction he had on her lips and sat up abruptly.

"Hey, where are you going so fast?" He reached for her and got hold of the sheet she was wrapping around herself. Did she know how seductive she looked with her hair sex teased, iridescent pearls gracing her neck and a bedsheet?

Eric threw the sheet on the floor. Goose bumps erupted on her skin and he lifted her against him making them both fall back on the bed.

"You have to go. I won't keep you." She was unable to keep her voice distant and cool. With him laying on top of her, she wanted to spread her legs and make love to him again.

"Lauren." He waited until she looked at him. "I'm in love with you." He seemed oblivious to how bad he shocked her as he rubbed his beard against the smooth skin on her cheek. "We should tell Shayla tonight."

"Whoa." He finally looked at her. "Tell her what?"

"About us. I'm not a man who sneaks around. I don't think I could stand to be in a room with you and not kiss or touch you. I want her to know how we feel." He slid his finger down her jaw bone while rotating his arousal against her. His lips got hold of her neck.

When she didn't respond, he lifted her face until their eyes met. "Okay. Maybe this is one-sided. How *do* you feel?"

"I-I . . ." He misinterpreted her hesitation. He got up and started dressing with his back to her.

Lauren scooted off the bed gathering the sheet as she went. She touched his arm and he turned.

Her voice was low and emotional. And sexy as hell. "I can't talk when you're naked. I can't breathe when you touch me. I forget all the things I want to remember when I'm with you. I'm scared. And I just don't think telling Shayla anything right now is the best idea. I need time to get used to this."

"How much time?" His bare feet curled into the thick carpet. He was home. They were perfect. Why couldn't she see it?

Lauren stepped back and caressed the bed with one hand, remembering. "I don't know. You . . . tonight . . . us . . . It's incredible." She shook her head. "No one could have told me I would feel or act this way."

Eric moved close behind her. She leaned into his broad chest. "What way?"

She took his hand from her waist and brought it around to her wildly beating heart. "This way." She turned and stared up into his eyes. "You don't have to say you love me. I don't have any preconceived-"

Three beeps split the air and Lauren jumped. Eric ripped the box off his waist and stared at the numbers.

Lauren backed away, grateful for the interruption. She was making a big mistake. Huge. Colossal. *He loved her.*

Lauren stepped farther back. She needed time. Time to evaluate her life, her goals. Her eyes snapped to his when she heard his voice.

"I'm not on call tonight. This had better be good." He breathed heavily and rubbed his beard. He still hadn't released her from his penetrating gaze and she stayed frozen in place. "Listen Rodney, it's okay. Give me the vitals." Eric listened then said, "You're going to have to do it. I'm thirty minutes away. Two more?" His voice rose incredulously. "I'm on my way." He hung up the phone.

Eric stuffed his shirt into the waist of his slacks and zipped. The jagged sound seemed to seal any further discussion. "Come here," he sat down on the edge of the bed.

Lauren slowly walked to him, and stood within the apex of his body. He closed his powerful thighs and held her firm. His hands rested on her sides, although the cream-colored sheet was not thick enough to keep the burn of his hands away.

"I've got one high-risk patient who fell and went into premature labor. Two more of my patients are on the way in, plus Rodney, my partner, has a few that have been in labor since early today. I have to leave now. But"—he drew her closer— "I'll be back tomorrow."

She nodded and kept her eyes riveted to the floor. Her heart swelled with love, yet something held her back from making the declaration that singed the tip of her tongue.

His finger tilted up her chin and she met his gaze. Their lips touched and she shivered when he spoke against her lips.

"I meant what I said. Loving you is getting to be very easy. I fantasize about spending my life with you. It's the scariest, most thrilling feeling I've ever had in my life." He sucked her lips one more time then drew away.

Lauren followed him down the stairs and held the door while he shrugged into his coat. "Goodnight," she called quietly as he walked onto the porch step.

"I'll call you tomorrow. Merry Christmas, Happy Kwanzaa, and Happy Hanukkah." She felt a tenderness inside her that he remembered.

"Eric?"

"Yeah, babe?" he answered, turning.

"Next time, wear the earring." She heard him laughing all the way to his daddy's big blue car.

Lauren finished cleaning up any evidence of her passionate evening and the powder off her bathroom floor by the time her mother and Shayla came in. She walked down the hall to the guest room. Her legs were sore, and so was her bottom from the fall against the car, but in the best way. She ached for him again. Would it always be like this?

"Mama?"

"Come in, baby." Chaney hummed as she undressed and handed her skirt to Lauren to hang while she slipped the padded hanger under her blouse.

"Did you have fun with Roscoe?"

"He was very nice. He asked me out for New Year's. I told him yes."

"Mama!" Lauren laughed. Her voice was teasing. "You didn't waste any time did you?"

"Honey, I'm middle aged. What am I waiting for? Either I want to or I don't. With Roscoe I do. It seems you had fun this evening, too."

Lauren blushed. Her mother was a youthful fifty something, but she hardly wanted to discuss her sex life with her.

"Don't wait too late to tell Shayla." Chaney grabbed hold of her cheeks and kissed them. "Merry Christmas. Peace be with you."

"And with you always." Lauren was engulfed in nostalgia. She hugged her mother and quietly left the room so she could have her private time to pray.

She tapped on Shayla's door and heard a muffled response. Lauren opened it and stuck her head inside. She felt so good after her evening with Eric, she didn't want to leave Shayla out. He had said he was in love with her. Lauren held her stomach as she sank on Shayla's bed. It's better to be direct with her than tell her when things are too far down the line. "Shayla, honey, could you get off the phone, I need to talk to you." She hung and looked at her.

"What is it, Ma?"

"Honey," nervous flutters wiggled in her stomach. "I've spent some time talking to your father."

"Hank?" Shayla eyed her suspiciously.

"No." Lauren laughed nervously. "No. Eric. Anyway, we . . . well he and I had a rather interesting—" Their *interesting* time came to mind and she crossed her legs licking her lips. *Now what?*

". . . Conversation, and we agreed that you should have the money for the college of your choice." Lauren struggled with how to bring up the subject of her and Eric's situation. "And you'll be glad to know that we're getting along better. In fact"—Lauren fidgeted with the strap on Shayla's purse— "we have feel—"

Shayla's eyebrows shot up and she raised her hands warding off her mother's words. Lauren stopped midsentence. "Ma, did you know I used to feel so lonely being adopted? I hated LeShay for a long time for leaving me." She smiled and Lauren felt the temperature in the room chill. "But now I have Eric. And you."

Lauren's fingers reflexively jerked against the strap and Shayla's purse overturned. Lauren gaped at the circular birth control pack that lay on the bed next to her leg. Several pills were missing. She yanked the pack off the bed and held it in her hand. "What is this?"

"It's birth control pills."

Lauren closed the door with her foot. She didn't want her mother to hear this conversation. "I know what they are, my question is why do you have them? Are you . . ." She breathed deeply. "Are you having sex?"

"I'm seventeen years old, Ma. I'm going to Emory next year."

"You didn't answer my question."

"I know!" Shayla burst out rising from the bed reaching for the pills as soon as Lauren slapped them on the bed.

"Shayla, you don't know what you're doing. Your whole future could change just like that." Lauren snapped her fingers in the air. "If you get pregnant."

"Ma, I'm not a kid anymore. I can't do anything without you around," she whined. "You're suffocating me."

"What?" Lauren whispered stunned.

"Don't do this. Do that," Shayla mimicked. "You always want me to do things your way."

"That isn't true. I let you make important decisions about your life. But I'm your mother. I have to be there to guide you. Everything I do is for you."

"I can't wait to go to college," Shayla muttered with a dark look in her eyes.

Lauren ignored the evil look. She was used to Shayla's moods. "There are benefits to abstaining from sex. I waited with your father . . ." She blanched. "Hank. I know what college is like. You'll meet a number of guys. You want to fall in love before you commit to something physical." *Is that what I've done?* Lauren shook the discomfiting thoughts from her head and reached for Shayla's hand. Shayla drew away before their hands met.

"Shayla, I have something to tell you about Eric and me."

"I want to go live with Eric." Shayla's words hit her like a two-ton truck. Lauren stared at her, unable to speak. Inside, her thoughts roared and she covered her mouth with her hand.

"What? Why?" The glow of her enjoyable evening burst like a tire on a semi. Shayla stared, her face a mask of defiance and anger. *It's all my fault,* Lauren thought desperately. *I should have been paying more attention to her. She needs me now more than ever.* "Honey, you don't need to do that. We can spend more time together." Lauren heard herself and couldn't stop the plea from entering her voice. "That's it. We'll go on a short vacation. Just the two of us."

"Ma! Stop! It's something *I* want to do. If you claim you let me make decisions, then I'm making this one. I only have this last semester of school, then the summer. I've lived with you forever. I want to get to know my father."

Lauren's heart hammered against her chest and she lowered her hand from her mouth. "You can stay here and see him whenever you want. You don't have to move."

Shayla started crying and Lauren wiped tears from her own eyes. Shayla wanted to leave her. Never since the adoption twelve years ago had they been apart for even one evening. Memories flooded her of Shayla at eight and ten asking if she could spend the night with her friends. The answer had always been the same. Why don't you have them come here? Lauren felt a awful disjointed feeling settle over her.

"But I want to." Shayla exploded. "I'm tired of being treated like a baby. I want to go live with my father." Something in Shayla's voice stopped her from pleading with her. Yet she couldn't stop the words from reverberating in her head. *Live with my father. I want to go live with my father.*

"All right." Lauren swallowed. "I don't mind." The lie stuck in her throat. "If he doesn't." Lauren walked out of Shayla's room in a state of shock, tears dripping off her face. She had just spent the most glorious night of her life with the man she loved and lost her daughter in the same evening.

She picked up the phone and dialed Eric's beeper number one last hope assailing her. He would never agree to this. It was ludicrous. He was single and had a very demanding schedule. There was no way he would be able to handle a teenager and his current lifestyle.

Her fingers shaking, she punched in her telephone number and the pound sign. Eric would never agree to this. He simply couldn't take her daughter away.

Chapter Twenty

Lauren stared across her desk at Herschel and Dakota Reynolds and marveled at their relationship. At six years old, Dakota was a genius. A miniature wizard. Herschel was handsome and doting, in search of financial security for himself and his child. He was also on a mission to find a mother for his daughter. His eyes twinkled everytime he looked at Dakota, and Lauren suppressed a sigh.

Two months and she had barely spoken to Shayla. She had seen her only a handful of times, and she missed her.

Terribly.

"Lauren," Herschel's high voice squeaked.

"Yes?"

"I asked you how much should I put in my savings account each month?"

"Oh, right." She silently berated her absent behavior. Lauren drew his chart from her desk and walked around to the visitors chair and sat. Dakota climbed on her lap and she held the girl while she pointed at the graph. "If you save one hundred dollars, in addition to the money you save on rent by being the courtesy officer in you apartment complex, then every month you should be depositing four hundred and fifty dollars. Within eighteen months you will have more than enough to make a down payment on a home for you and Dakota.''

She tickled the girl who broke in saying, ''That's eight thousand one hundred dollars. Right, Miss Lauren?''

''That's right, sweetheart. Why don't you go get the newspaper from Pam and bring it to me.''

''Okay.'' Dakota hopped off her lap and landed with a thud, then took off running.

''Don't run.'' She couldn't stop the gentle rebuff from coming out of her mouth. Nostalgic memories of Shayla at that age resurfaced.

''You're so good with her.'' Herschel smiled taking her hand. ''Why don't you come to lunch with us and let me convince you how much we need you?''

Lauren withdrew it, squaring her shoulders, fixing him with a professional smile. ''I already have plans.''

''Yes, she does.'' The chart slipped from her fingers as the familiar voice she had been wanting to hear tingled up her spine when she rose.

Lauren stared at Eric who blocked the entrance to her office with his broad shoulders. He looked so good. But so tired. He walked into the room and stole all the air. His hungry eyes searched hers and she looked down, noticing Herschel staring between the two of them.

''Herschel Reynolds, Eric Crawford.'' His name came out of her mouth breathlessly as if she had just run a marathon. Nervously, Lauren rubbed her hands together and stumbled around the guest chair.

''I've been trying to reach you,'' he said.

''I've been busy.''

''Too busy to pick up the phone and let somebody know you're okay?''

"Eric." She glanced at her client then back at him.

Eric walked over to the man and took his outstretched hand. He pumped it, practically dragging him to the door. Dakota burst in and handed Lauren the paper. She gathered her computer and looked up at the adults.

"Come on, Daddy. They need grown-up time."

Eric dropped to one knee and extended his hand. She shook it solemnly. "Thank you. You're a very perceptive little lady."

"Yes, I know. Bye, Miss Lauren."

"Goodbye, Dakota. Thank you for understanding, Herschel." Lauren saw them to the elevator and stalked back to her office.

"Eric Crawford, just who do you think you are? You have no right coming in my office—Eric?"

"I'm over here." He waved his hand from the couch. Lauren walked over ready to charge him up, but what she saw pulled at her heartstrings. Eric rested his head against the armrest of the couch, one foot bracing his body on the floor, the other stretched off the end of the sofa. His eyes were closed. When he opened them, they were bloodshot red.

"Eric, what's the matter?" She resisted rubbing his face with her hand, and taking him in her arms. "Do you need another list of Shayla's necessities?"

"No," he sighed, reaching for her hand pulling her down beside him. "Shayla does her own shopping for her personal items. I came to see you."

"Oh. Well then, what's up?" She tried to keep her voice cheerful, but being this close to him was wreaking havoc on her system. Her breathing shallowed and she remembered all the pleasures his hands brought her. She had been hoarse for a week after their evening together.

"I want to know why you've been ignoring my calls, and why you left my parents' house Saturday when you knew I was coming by."

His fingers gripped her wrist, not tight enough to hurt, but enough so she couldn't get away.

Lauren laughed and tried to shake her wrist from his hand. He kept his grip firm and she stopped trying. He laid it open on his chest and she felt the distinct thump of his heart against her palm.

"Mother and Roscoe had plans and mother needed a ride. I thought it would be rude to come all that way and not say hello to your folks. I couldn't stay," she lied. "I—I wasn't trying to avoid you."

"It's a good thing you do other things better than lie." His thumb caressed her palm. "You damn near hurtled over the bushes getting back to your car. Your new nieces were playing with the video camera and have it all on tape."

Lauren couldn't resist a little giggle remembering how she had grown weak thinking of seeing him. Sure she had damn near hurdled the bush. So what, she would never confess to him that he made her do it. Instead of seeing him, she had gone for the complete workup at Geoffrey's, hoping it would ease some of the tension away. It hadn't. Chills tingled her spine, the memory of how she had turned to jelly in his arms still fresh in her mind.

Lauren cupped her chin directing her sight to the birthmark on his arm that began it all. "Eric Crawford, you're telling tales."

"Am I?" he asked and gathered a fistful of her suit and pulled until his mouth clamped over hers. Sharp pelts of desire stabbed through her and Lauren opened her mouth for him. Kissing him was like going home. It was familiar and good and licked at the yearning she had kept at bay.

His tongue mated with hers in a slow, nasty dance that she had come to know strictly as Eric's kiss. It would never be duplicated, never outdone. Lauren moaned into his mouth and felt his fingers deftly undo the buttons on her jacket. It was on. There was no turning back.

"Wait, the door." Lauren hurried and turned the lock in the chamber and forwarded her phone. She pressed the DO NOT DISTURB—IN CONFERENCE button, and short of a national emergency, she knew Pam wouldn't ring her.

Making love to Eric crowded any other thoughts from her mind and she rounded the back of the couch to stand in front of him. He had raised to a sitting position and pulled her by the back of her thighs closer to him. Her one-piece vest-jacket hung open and he pressed his lips to her flesh between her breasts and naval.

Lauren swayed and clutched his head. Every part of her had turned to liquid as she stood before the man she loved in high heels, his face against her midriff. Lauren reached behind herself and unzipped her skirt. She had a surprise for him.

"You remembered," he growled his tongue darting into her naval, his fingers easing the garter belt down.

"Yes," she moaned, when he let the skirt fall. "I remembered." With quick skill, the garter belt and clips lay at her feet. The tiny panties were moist and easy to remove. Lauren heard her ragged breathing as he slid his hands between her thighs and pulled her bottom forward, her center accessible to his probing tongue.

Lauren swooned from the sensation and her knees buckled. He was so good at giving her pleasure. His tongue slid from her and she watched through slit eyes the provocative thrust of pink meeting dark curls.

"Eric, I want you." Lauren wrapped her arms around his head. She had nothing else to hold onto. Her lace bra hung on one breast, the other side carelessly cast aside by his teeth. He sat back making her lean over, nursing it. He drank as if a potent elixir was coming from the tiny dark pores.

Lauren's knees finally gave out and she landed in his lap. She cupped his erection and she closed her hand gently over it. His hand covered hers and made her squeeze harder. His face was against her neck when he spoke. "I don't know how many nights I've done this to myself. But I'll be damned if tonight is going to be one of them again.''

"It won't be, darling. I promise." Lauren reached between them and unbuckled his belt pulling it slowly from the loops of his pants. Next, she unbuttoned his waist. Then she worked the jagged zipper down. Eric was so full, he was pressed against his stomach bound by his colored briefs. She reached inside and freed him, squeezing up and down in slow arduous motions. The desire to kiss him overwhelmed her. And she did. Right before he nearly bolted from the couch when her mouth covered his erect tip.

"Oh, sh—'' he cursed, his thighs jerking, his hands filling with her hair. Lauren didn't stop even as he pressed her down, her mouth more than full of him. She sucked and licked and a couple of times squeezed the full sacks of his testicles, which made him cry out in a harsh bark of laughter. Her own desire escalated and she knew her release was near.

Eric lifted her from him like she was a rag doll and sat her next to him. He stood, dug in the pocket and pulled out a condom. When he was sheathed and naked from the waist down, he sat and pulled her into position on top of him.

He made her sweat. Lauren contracted against him, her walls squeezing until he cried out. Her legs ached from straddling his body, but it was all good. She didn't care. All that mattered as she rode him, thrusting and pumping, was how he felt and how she felt. He didn't touch her breasts or her lips. His head was thrown back his eyes half closed as he held her hips, pulling her closer as he pushed deeper into her. The movements were fast and hard and a familiar burn started down low, creeping up. They moved faster, the sweat on their thighs slapping like waves against a reef. Lauren raised higher, pushing down, holding his shoulders. Then he struck her with his finger tips, right between the legs. And she screamed. Tears streamed down her face as she came. Again. And again. And again.

Eric gave one long curse and he met her in sweet oblivion.

He grasped her around her back and rocked unable to let her go, unwilling to end their joyous ride.

Hot tears slid down his neck. They weren't the tears of a woman who had just been made love to. They were sad tears that had her body shaking and him worried. He soothed her until she could speak.

"Why, Eric? Why did you let Shayla come live with you?"

There it was. It had kept them apart for two months. Sixty days of cold showers, wet dreams, and a tender palm. She had finally asked the question that must have been tearing her up inside. He unbuttoned his shirt and wrapped it around her shoulders. When she was partially covered, he slid on his underwear and slacks leaving them half undone. He had to tell her the truth.

"Because I couldn't stand to lose either of you."

Lauren dropped her head, tiny teardrops sliding off her chin. He held her hands as they sat side by side overlooking cold Atlanta. "Lauren, I couldn't tell her no. I just found her." He tightened his grip on her hand. "I thought we could work this out together. I figured that if she came to stay with me for a while, eventually she would miss you and we would all be together. We need you."

Lauren shook her head no, and his frustration grew. Short of getting on his knees, he didn't know what else would convince her of his love. He had been there and thought he had her convinced. Apparently not.

Shayla presented no problem as far as he was concerned. They should just tell her, and she would accept their love. But Lauren had this crazy idea that Shayla would lose it if she found out.

"Lauren, you're raising obstacles where there aren't any. Shayla will be fine with this."

"No she won't, Eric. You don't know her like I do. It's

me she hates right now. Not you. She would blame me for everything.'' She stood, his shirt dangling off her arms. ''Eric, I've always protected her. Her needs came first and I can't think any other way.''

She turned to face him. ''You're at a great advantage right now. She loves you unconditionally. Me, she's angry with because I control her. I can't lose more.'' Eric tried to take her into his arms. The fact that she avoided his touch, gathering her clothes together, made him feel worse than he did before he came into her office. He followed her to the tiny bath and stood outside while she freshened up.

Eric accepted his shirt from her outstretched hand and tried to peer inside the door before she closed it. Frustrated, he growled and jerked his shirt on. Her scent was all over him and he inhaled deeply. The sharp pain took his breath away. His hand slid to his right side and he felt the sore spot. Ever since he had been here with her, he had forgotten the pain. The headache and allover body ache was gone for the time being. Lauren was the salve to soothe his beastly mood.

She came out of the bathroom and sat at her desk, her eyes averted from him. Every hair was in place and her mood was distant. How could he love this woman? One minute she was crying on his shoulder and the next she was the ice princess.

He took his turn in the bathroom and fastened the button on the cuff of his shirt.

''Can I use this?'' he asked, indicating her toothbrush. He had kissed, licked, and sucked every intimate part of her body, he doubted she would mind.

''Go ahead,'' she said softly, watching. Eric used many of her personal items. Her wash cloth, and face lotion, comb, and brush all groomed a part of him.

When he was done, he came out and braced his hands on either side of her chair. ''True love is hard to find. Are you going to risk losing it?''

"I love Shayla," she whispered.

He tilted her chin up. "And I love you."

"I'm glad you stopped by."

He straightened and walked around her desk, a feeling of foreboding overcoming him. Especially when she reached for her purse. Extracting her checkbook, she scribbled quickly and tore the check out. "Here's my child support for Shayla. I would have mailed it but since you're here, you saved me a trip to the post office."

Eric lost his temper. "I'm not taking your damn money." His fingers closed over her hand. He turned it palm up and with deceptive calm took the check. He crunched it, then threw it against the desk, where it popped up and hit her in the chest.

"I see what you're trying to do and if this is the way you want it, then fine. I'm not going to be the go-between for you and Shayla anymore. If you two don't want to act like mother and daughter that's up to you. If you don't want to see me, that's up to you, too. But don't cheapen my love for you by giving me your damned money."

He banged his knuckles on the desk. "You've got what you want. I'll leave you alone."

Eric stalked from the office, and punched the button for the elevator. Lauren was impossible! Maybe forgetting about a personal relationship was best. She would make him gray with her obstinate attitude.

He made it to his car before a jolt of pain tore through his side again. He resisted doubling over. There it was again. This time it didn't go away so quickly. It lingered like little knives slicing in, not as strong as the first one but just as painful. Eventually it subsided and he turned the key in the engine and directed his car toward the center. *How can I be in love with someone so headstrong, contumacious, inflexible, and bull-headed?*

Eric laid his head against the head rest in his Mercedes and blinked slowly. After a day like today, he deserved a break. He took the exit for home. I'm too tired to ask for donations anyway. He drove home not looking forward to his warm, lonely bed.

Chapter Twenty-One

Shayla lay across her double bed, patting the empty space by her side. "My father won't be back for hours, Malik. We have the whole house to ourselves." She loved the hungry look in Malik's eyes. Soon she wouldn't be a virgin anymore. She quivered in anticipation.

"Did you hear something?" Shayla asked, sitting up on the bed pulling her top down over her bare breasts.

"I didn't hear nothing," he said, anxiously. "Come on Shayla," he rose off the bed the buckle of his belt clinking together as he unfastened it. "Are we gonna do it or what?"

Shayla's face registered horror.

"Think again, son. You pull that thing out, you won't go home with it." Eric stood behind the boy and laid a powerful hand on his shoulder. He looked at Shayla and barked, "Downstairs, now."

She had to squeeze past him to get out the door. He averted his gaze from her near nakedness. Anger rose in him and Eric assisted the door shut with his foot. He had to close his eyes and count to ten or else he was going to kill this kid. Eric waited and increased the pressure in his fingers. The boy yelped in pain. *Good. That sounds good.* Eric turned him to face him.

"Rule number one, this is the last time you're ever going to cross the door of this room. Take a good look because you won't see it again. Rule two, if you want to see my daughter, you ask me first. Rule three, if I ever catch you in this house and I'm not here, God help you, boy, because you won't make it home on those legs you got now. Understood?"

"Yes, sir," came the quivering reply.

"What's your name, son?"

"Malik Chambers."

"How long have you known my daughter?"

"All my life, but we haven't been seeing each other long," he reassured then shook like a leaf on a tree. Fear widened his eyes. Bad choice of words.

"That's the wrong answer son. I don't care if you knew her from the moment she took her first breath, it still isn't long enough for me. Now if you want to see her, you start at the front door, not her bedroom door. I won't repeat myself."

"No, sir."

"Go home before I change my mind about letting you *walk* out of here." Eric glared at the kid and watched as he hastily grabbed his coat and rushed down the stairs three at a time until he was out the house.

Eric leaned against the white desk chair he had just bought to complete Shayla's room. His daughter was having sex. He groaned and wiped his hands through his hair. How would Lauren handle this? Would she yell, or ground her? Would she talk reasonably with the two of them or would she talk with the boys parents? *I have no idea what I'm doing.* Eric walked down the stairs and shut the front door, which had been left ajar by the young boy's hasty exit. He stepped down into the living room and confronted a brooding Shayla.

"What did you have to embarrass me for?"

Eric stared, stupefied. "Shayla, you're not going to sleep around in this house."

"Where should I go, to the park?" she retorted. "You're just like my mother. I can't do anything." She got up and stalked toward the stairs.

Eric's headache returned but he ignored it. "You sit down now." His voice cut through the air and Shayla stopped in silent debate. "We're going to talk about this like adults."

"Another lecture." Shayla rolled her eyes in her head, crossing her arms. She flopped back down on the couch.

"No, it's not. You start first. Tell me why you think I should let you sleep around."

"I'm not sleeping around. Malik and I have known each other for years."

"Okay. So you two have a plan if you get pregnant with his baby."

"I'm not going to get pregnant."

"Right," he said, tapping his finger to his temple as if to remind himself of something. "You're on the pill. So I suppose good friend Malik is going to take care of you if he gives you any diseases. Like AIDS, gonorrhea, herpes . . ."

"No. I mean he doesn't have anything like that and I'm still a virgin so I can't give him anything."

"Is he?" Eric knew this was a bombshell and that she was hurt that he asked but he knew of no other way to reach her. "Do you honestly know?" He sat by her on the sofa. "Are you willing to risk your life for a few minutes of pleasure because you want to believe you're not sleeping with everyone he's slept with?"

"I don't know." Her admission rocked her and she lowered her head crying. Eric gathered her to his shoulder, the same one her mother had cried on earlier. He had a thing for beautiful crying women.

"Shayla, you have time. I'm not saying Malik isn't the one,

I'm just saying you don't know enough about him to be making this decision right now."

Her nodding meant he had won one battle. He wasn't so sure about the war.

"We need some house rules." Eric waited for her to stop sniffling before continuing. "Rule one, no unexpected company, unless it's family. Two, no personal entertaining in our rooms."

Shayla opened her mouth to protest and he held up his hands pointing to himself saying, "I can live with that. Two more," he said to her moody stare.

"We make out a written schedule for the week and leave numbers where each can be reached, and last, we both work."

"What?" she drew back, incredulous.

"That's right. If I have to work, so do you. Besides, I think working at the center will go a long way to helping you get into Emory."

"Eric, I go to school." She leaned forward presenting her case. "I have to study, too, and all you do is go to the office, see a couple of patients and come home. It's not fair that I should be pulling more weight than you."

Eric snorted a laugh, then cleared his throat. "Shayla, if I were you, I would remember that I'm grounded for the next month for having Malik here without asking. You don't want me to accompany you to classes for the rest of the semester to make sure you have reputable friends do you?"

"No!" She shook, disgust marking her beautiful features. "As it is, you already control my life, driving me to school everyday. I might as well be riding the yellow bus. We practically live in Tennessee and I still don't have my car."

"We can rectify that. You could transfer," he suggested, holding in a full-fledged laugh at her wide-eyed, open mouth stare.

"All my friends go to my school. I'm a senior . . ."

"Well then, you've made some very strong arguments for

calling your mother and asking about your car privileges haven't you?''

Eric carried the phone from the kitchen and laid it on the couch. "I'll be back in a few minutes. You have time to call her now."

Eric didn't wait for her to respond. Shayla sat defiantly in the corner of the couch, turned away from the phone. Eric knew she would call, and when he closed the door to his room, he was pleased to hear that she was at least grumbling. It wouldn't be long before she dialed.

Swallowing some Tylenol, he flopped his briefcase on his bed and extracted a full folder on the finances for the youth center. The numbers hadn't jived for the past three months and something told him if they didn't get some sizable donations soon, they were in serious trouble.

Chapter Twenty-Two

That couldn't be right. Eric configured the numbers again. From all indications, the center was over one hundred and fifty thousand dollars in the red. Some deficit was expected but not this much.

"What are you doing?" Shayla asked from the door.

Dropping his glasses on the desk, Eric drew his hand over his face and stretched. "Trying to figure out where to get money for the center."

"Do you still have a temperature?" she asked importantly.

He couldn't hide anything from her. During their stay together, they had come to know one another and respect their similarities and differences. Shayla wasn't a morning person. She hated talking before she had her first cup of coffee. Whereas he liked to jog and read the paper before dawn. He loved pasta and she didn't eat meat. She loved basketball and even had a decent hook shot, for someone so short.

She bristled when he called her short-stuff at one of their family Thursday night basketball games. Shayla had changed his family, too. No longer did just the men play on the courts Thursday evenings. Now it was co-ed. Everybody got to play.

He loved her. He just wished he could have known her since she was a child. Perhaps in an earlier time and place, he and Lauren would have been married and had more children. Maybe he would have four or five Shayla's running around. He groaned and smiled. For right now, one was enough. And they way things looked, he was very unsure of their future together.

"No, I think it's gone." His forehead still burned, but he ignored it. A cold wasn't something you called a doctor over. "How did your talk with your mother go?"

"She really sounded liked she missed me." Saddened for a moment she raised her head. "She didn't ask me to come home though."

"Do you want to?"

"No," she said, hastily. "I like living here with you. Don't you like having me here?"

"Of course. I was just thinking that you might want to spend a weekend at home with your mom soon." Eric knew that would make Lauren very happy. She had been so miserable today. He hated to think of her alone. He wanted them all to be together.

"Yeah, I might do that tomorrow. Yeah, she wants me to."

"I know she sings at the club Friday. But I'm sure she would enjoy you two spending time together. It would probably be really boring around here anyway. I've got so much to do this weekend."

"At the center?"

"No. My car needs a tune-up." He fidgeted, thinking of the woman he loved. He couldn't hold it in any longer. He had to tell Shayla of his feelings for Lauren.

"I've been thinking about something and I thought you and I should talk about it."

Shayla shrugged and sat on the couch.

Nervously, Eric rubbed his hands together and came around

his desk. It seemed as if the heat in the room had intensified and he watched his daughter watching him.

"Uh, Shayla, since this thing with Malik happened, I've been thinking about my own actions and I can't say one thing and do another. I've met someone, and I want you to know about her."

Shayla's spine straightened and she crossed her arms over her chest and stared at him.

Eric chanced a look at her then pushed on. His voice took on a tender quality and his heart thundered against his ribs. The dull pain was still in his side but he pushed it to the back of his thoughts. "She's incredible. She's smart, and beautiful, talented, and a really wonderful person. She has a big heart and I'm in love with her." It felt so good to get the words out, Eric sighed heavily.

"How come I haven't met her?" Shayla asked in an accusatory voice.

"Honey, you have." Eric sat beside her and took her hand. Her gray eyes were confused, then scared. He hoped to lessen the shock. "It's someone you've know for a long time. Someone you already love. It's your mother, Shayla. I'm in love with Lauren."

Shayla covered her mouth then her face with her hands. Eric could hear her breathing faster and she kept looking at him then away. Yet she said nothing. His discomfort increased and he grew more nervous. "Tell me what you think about me loving your mom."

"It's cool. I'm sure she'll really like that. I better go to bed."

Eric rose disappointed and watched Shayla walk out of his office and into her room. The door closed with a bang and he stared, unsure what to do next. He wanted to shout from the roof tops. He wanted to sing, dance even. Instead he stood alone in his office, and rested his hands on his hips. *Somehow, I expected more than this.*

* * *

Lauren arrived at the club twenty minutes late. Jimmy B met her at the back entrance anxiety pulsing from his every pore. "The headliner is late! What kind of mess . . ." She knew what he wanted to say and for once agreed with him. The musicians milled in the hall, smoking cigarettes, waiting for her. They were on in less than five minutes. Usually they were warmed up by now, but she had been unavoidably delayed.

Ever since she had spoken to Shayla the day before, she had been fighting the urge to cry. Yesterday, was the first time in a long time they actually had a conversation and were able to laugh. She knew it was Eric's doing. *Don't think about him. Don't think about him.*

Lauren stumbled, and dropped her garment bag. The curse she gave brought everyone in the hall, including Jimmy, to an utter, screeching halt. She didn't curse. She was picking up Eric's bad habits. Under the curious stares of the band, her chin began to quiver and tears fell.

PeeWee took her hand and led her into the closet-sized dressing room. He kicked the door closed with a resounding thud making it clear no one was to enter.

"Talk to me," he commanded, and sat her on the lone chair in the room.

"I'm going to be okay, thank you, PeeWee. I just need a few minutes to get myself together."

"It's the guy from last time isn't it?"

"No," she lied, partly because she knew PeeWee would be a bloodhound searching for Eric.

"Aw, right," he nodded affirmatively. She was sure he saw through her thin lie. "Get dressed. I'll stall Jimmy."

"Thank you. Oh," her voice cracked, and he turned from the door to look at her. Lauren inhaled then let out the breath slowly. "Just in case he turns up, don't let him in, okay?"

"Got it." He made a shooting motion with his hand that made her slightly uneasy.

Lauren took the stage and sang with all her heart. Every sad love song she could think of tumbled from her lips and she poured her soul into them. The audience didn't care. They cheered long and loud demanding two encores.

The set ended and despite everything she had said to PeeWee, she still searched every corner of the club for him.

There were no gray eyes penetrating hers as she swayed to the music. No walnut brown skin to caress when she got back to the dressing room, and no delicious lips to kiss making every inch of her feel desirable.

He hadn't come, and her heart wept. Lauren held the tears at bay until she reached the dressing room and when she walked inside, she let them fall.

A knock at the door sent her flying to it. Lauren yanked it open, expecting to find Eric on the other side.

Instead, Jimmy B grinned at her. "Lauren, I have a surprise for you. Meet Jake Watson. He's with Blackbelt records out of New York. Honey, he wants you to make him a record."

Lauren took the outstretched hand and met the curious gaze of Mr. Jake Watson.

Chapter Twenty-Three

"It sounds interesting, Mr. Watson, but I'll have to think about it." Lauren assessed the man who sat across from her. The talented record mogul represented some of the most successful singers in the business.

He had come to Atlanta in the February cold to see her and she was grateful. Happy. And scared.

Lauren ceased the incessant tapping of her foot and met his steady gaze. "If I accept your offer, I won't be able to move to New York. I have a teenage daughter."

"A lot of our people have families, Lauren. We work with them and you would be no different. Besides a move to New York is not imminent. I'd like to get you there just to tape a demo. If we like what we see"—he opened his hands face up—"then we talk business." Watson leaned forward, taking her hand. "But from what I saw tonight, you shouldn't have any problem, you were fantastic."

Lauren withdrew her hand carefully and scooted to the edge of the booth. The whirlwind of emotions had her spinning faster than a top. A demo, then a possible contract! What next, Carnegie Hall?

Too much was happening at once. Lauren stepped down from the elevated booth and presented her hand to Mr. Watson who kissed the back. "Thank you, Mr. Watson. I appreciate your consideration." Lauren picked up the business card he slid across the table. "I'll give you a call next week."

"Good." He nodded thoughtfully. "But Lauren, let me give you a word of advice. You're hot and I see serious potential." The smile reached his lips but neglected to warm his eyes. "Don't take too long."

Lauren nodded and walked away from the table. A record! How was she going to tell Shayla her mother might be the next woman on the top-forty billboard charts?

PeeWee waited patiently for her as she practically flew down the hall toward the dressing room. "You had a call," he said.

Lauren grasped the big mans forearm her heart pounding.

"Who?"

"Me."

She pivoted slowly, the masculine voice caressing her. It was what she had been wishing and waiting for for days. It took only three steps and she was in his arms.

Eric wasted no time lifting her off her feet against his strong body where she had found hours of comfort and pleasure. The door to the dressing room closed discreetly and Lauren kissed him with a burning hunger that was insatiable.

She let her tongue explore at leisure and enjoyed tasting him, making her feelings known with each pass over his lips, that she missed him. Eric returned her passion, his hands seeking all the places they enjoyed the last time they were together. He guided their bodies nearer until only the material of their clothes separated them.

Eric rested her bottom on the table and fitted himself comfortably between her legs, his wide hands supporting her back. Lauren grasped his cheeks, her lips seeking his, her tongue wrapping itself around his, their kiss soulful and deep. Desire abounded. The rush in her ears, the boom in her chest, and her watery legs were all physical indications that she missed him. Wanted him. But the volcanic explosion of her heart let her know that she loved him.

It was moments before they separated and only because her head was pressed at an odd angle against the mirror while he tended to her breast which had been freed during their fiery stroking.

"Eric, my neck," she groaned.

"It sure tastes good to me." He plastered his lips to her and made a believer out of her. Lauren giggled at the love bites he gave until she heard her moans echo in the small room.

"I mean it now," she said, without conviction. "We have to stop."

His lips vacated the space and Lauren touched the swollen flesh and giggled. Eric stood straight, but continued to caress her legs in slow pleasure filled circles. Lauren began talking excitedly. "You'll never guess what happened to me tonight. After the set was over, I came back here and got a big, I mean, huge, gargantuan surprise." She hopped off the table.

Eric looked at her quizzically. "You hit the lottery?" She giggled, before kissing him. "Almost. Wait," she grabbed her coat and scarf.

"I want to tell you and Shayla together. Let's go to your place."

Eric responded to her enthusiasm with a smoldering kiss. "Those are words I've been dying to hear." He helped her slide her coat on.

She turned, staying close. "This means so much to me that you came today. I did a lot of thinking after I talked to Shayla— what's the matter?" Panic assaulted her when she turned to see him clutching the table, his face ashen. Her heart thundered as she took steps toward him and touched his cheek. He was hot. But his eyes shone brilliantly. Fear gripped her. "Eric, what's wrong?"

"I'm just excited to see you so happy. Come home with me, Lauren." Lauren stepped close and let him drape his arm over her shoulder. His weight sank on her shoulder and they walked slowly to the car. "It's a beautiful night isn't it?"

"You're beautiful."

He slid into the passenger side of his car. "Do you mind driving? I'm tired."

Alarm bells rang again and Lauren stared at his face in the dim light. Something was wrong. He was never sick. Not since she'd known him. Not since she'd fallen in love with him.

Lauren started the car and drove.

He seemed to be sleeping and her heart expanded. His five o'clock shadow had filled in a bit and he looked more handsome than ever. Lauren reached over and lightly touched the back of his hand, which rested on his thigh. He grasped hers with a strength that radiated through her and her fears were dispelled. He was fine. Probably just a cold.

"I can't wait to see Shayla." Lauren returned her eyes to the road. The little car darted in and out of traffic smoothly. She loved it too. "I appreciate you having her call me Monday. She said she was going to spend the weekend at your house, something about being grounded for talking on the phone too much."

Lauren turned off the interstate at her exit and drove in silence. Eric sat up and stared intently out the car window. "I don't have a problem with you grounding her, Eric. I just want you to know."

"She's supposed to be at your house tonight."

Lauren slammed on the brakes, sending the car into a short slide. She grabbed his arm, worry creeping through her.

"Shayla told me that she was going to stay home with you." Lauren tried to quell the panic that welled within her as she stared out the front window oblivious to the cars that whizzed by.

"Lauren, she told me specifically that she was spending the weekend with you. She said you invited her."

"I did." Lauren lowered her voice. She was practically screaming. "She said no."

Eric patted her shoulder reassuringly. "It's probably just a misunderstanding. Let's go to your place."

He grabbed the phone and dialed.

"Who are you calling?"

"My house."

She drove, hoping Shayla would answer. Eric's voice was deceptively calm. "Shayla, if you're there pick up." Lauren prayed silently. "Call me in the car when you get this message."

They hit the driveway and she screeched to a halt.

"I'm going inside." Lauren cut off the headlights. She slipped on the slick pavement, running for the front door. The house was pitch black and she knew immediately, Shayla was not there.

Eric followed, but slower. Lauren raced past him up the stairs calling Shayla's name, but received no response.

"She's not here." Lauren came down the stairs to face him. "What did you say to her when you grounded her?"

"I didn't ground her. When I found her with Malik in her room, I just threatened her and him."

"Malik! What are you saying?"

"What do you think?" His voice had taken on an edge and he massaged his eyes looking totally pissed.

"I don't think anything. Shayla and Malik have been child-hood friends forever. They've been going in each others rooms since they were children. I don't appreciate you insinuating anything—"

"I found them on her bed getting ready to make love Monday."

"What!"

"Get your head out of the clouds, Lauren. Childhood friends grow up. They have adult urges. These two obviously have you fooled."

Lauren wanted to scream. He was making this up. It had to be another Malik. Shayla and Malik were friends. Memories of Christmas Eve snapped into her head. Malik kissing Shayla. The two of them in his room playing video games. Was that all they were playing? Or were they playing her for a fool? Lauren tamped down her anger and fear. They still didn't know where Shayla was.

"I'm nobody's fool. I have eyes. I can see. And these kids are just friends. I'm calling Rissa."

Lauren hurried to the phone with Eric hot on her heels.

"Rissa, is Malik Jr. home? We're looking for Shayla and we can't seem to find her."

They both put their ears to the phone listening to Rissa's response.

"Malik's butt is grounded for getting in late Monday night. He claimed he had to catch busses and trains from wherever he was, but I told him I didn't care if he had to sprout wings. He should have been home under curfew."

Eric grimaced and put the phone fully on his ear. "He was at my house and I tossed him out. I didn't know he didn't have a ride home." Eric shrugged at Lauren's shocked expression.

"You practically live in Tennessee! Hold on ..." They could hear her calling Malik's name in the distance. She came back to the phone breathless. "He's not here. I think they're together."

"Why do you say that?" From Eric's tone Lauren covered the scared moan that kept escaping from her lips.

Rissa's voice lowered. "Well, because I found the phone directory opened to hotels and the *Days Inn* by Lauren's house had a check mark by it."

"They're at a hotel." It wasn't a question and Eric leaned

his head heavily on the cabinet in front of him. His eyes averted from Lauren's wide ones.

"Rissa, when I find your son, I'm going to kill him."

"Not if I get my hands on him first. Let me speak to Lauren, I know she's probably having a coronary."

Lauren took the phone from his outstretched hand. She mumbled a few cursory words then replaced the receiver. She hurried to the garage door and opened it.

Her gaze was cold when she looked at Eric. "Her car is gone. Eric, what in the name of God did you say to her to make her run off?"

Chapter Twenty-Four

Eric was pissed. "I'm going after her." Fuming, wasn't enough to describe his anger. His jaw muscles bunched out from where he had his teeth clenched. Lauren literally jumped when he pounded his fist on the counter and growled. He was angry beyond anything she'd ever seen and she was scared. For Malik.

"She was perfectly all right this week. I asked her did she want to talk about it and she said no, she wanted to go to sleep."

"Wait! Where are you going?"

They were back outside in the cold. The temperature seemed to have dropped twenty degrees and their breath puffed then evaporated with short, fast blasts.

"I'm going to that hotel and I'm going to have some Malik butt for dinner." He stalked around the car and slid into the driver seat. Lauren tipped carefully on the high heels, afraid of falling, still wondering what could have sent Shayla into the arms of her friend. Was it attraction? Or were they really in love? It was possible. Anything was possible. She loved Shayla's father, and that had seemed impossible only months ago.

Eric gunned the high performance vehicle out of the driveway and was on the main highway within minutes. His eyes were a brilliant gray, brighter than she'd ever seen. If she had thought he didn't love Shayla, she sure would have changed her mind now. He was driving as if demons were chasing him. "Eric, slow down. The hotel is over there," she pointed to the other side of the major road they were on. "We're going to miss the turn."

She needn't have said any more. The tires squealed in protest of the abrupt change of direction and soon traction took hold. Lauren, jostled around by the quick movement spotted Shayla's car.

"Stop. They're here."

Lauren thought Eric was going to jump out of the car, but he sat with his eyes closed for a few seconds. "Let me handle this, Lauren."

"She's my daughter, too. I have something to say."

"No dammit. They out-right defied me, and I'm going to handle it. No discussion." Fury raged through her as he opened the door and stepped out.

"You wait just a minute!" Lauren struggled to get out of the seat belt. She yanked open the door, and slid on a patch of ice before catching up with Eric. They were at the sidewalk when he came to an abrupt halt. They both stared.

Shayla and Malik were coming toward them unaware of their presence. Lauren put a cautious hand on Eric's arm but he was stronger and faster than her.

Eric saw red. Malik had his arm around Shayla's shoulder talking in her ear. Like lovers. Distantly he heard Lauren call his name but nothing was going to stop him from beating the boy to a pulp. He reached the young couple, startling them.

Fear, then recognition, then terror struck the eyes of the young man who yelped and tried to escape Eric's vice grip.

Eric had him slammed high on the wall when Lauren and Shayla reacted. "Eric, stop! Please don't hurt him."

"Daddy please . . . nothing happened."

Their screams and pleas did nothing to deter him.

"What did I tell you, boy?" he asked menacingly shaking him as if he were a dime-store rag doll.

"Do-don't come back—"

"That's right. I didn't mean go somewhere else. I meant don't ever touch her." He enunciated each word with a thrust of the boys body against the hotel wall. "That's my daughter whom I love very—" Pain tore through Eric's side and he fell against the boy waiting for it to subside. It seared him like a hot poker, and he grasped the boy harder.

He stepped back and breathed heavily. "I love Shayla, and you or nobody else is going to take advantage of her."

Sweating profusely, he ignored the tugging at his arm and swung it off.

"Daddy ple-ease," Shayla begged crying. "Please don't hurt him. Please, daddy it's my fault. I love you, too. Please dad-ddy don't—"

"I'm going to teach this boy a lesson."

"Eric!" Lauren's sobs penetrated his ears and he was moving very fast. His fist connected with something very soft. Not at all what he expected. He felt the burning pain again. Something was wrong.

And then it was dark.

He was flying in the light reaching out his hand wanting to touch her. Her voice called to him and he moved his lips answering. Eric slid into consciousness slowly, unobserved by his brothers who huddled at the door.

Listening to their discussions proved easy as they did little to disguise what they were saying.

"Do you think the boy's mother will sue?"

"Who knows. Clarissa Chambers is a widely respected attorney. Forget that she's Lauren's friend. Eric knocked her kid unconscious. His dad is a cop." This drew murmurs.

"What about Lauren? Did you see her eye? Eric is in deep sh . . ."

What did I do to her eye? Eric struggled to open his eyes and look around. He knew his brother Michael was there. And he recognized Edwin's voice, too. But he knew if he were there, all of his family was near.

"What happened to Lauren's eye?" Five sets of gray eyes converged on him and he stared back.

"About time," Julian said.

"You've been out for exactly six hours and twenty three minutes." Michael said. "You had appendicitis—and no rupture. You're in good shape, considering. Lauren called the ambulance and you were rushed into surgery immediately. Despite how you treated her." Ten gray eyeballs looked at him disapprovingly.

"What happened to Lauren?" Eric asked again. His brothers stared between each other.

It took all his strength, but he grabbed the covers and threw them back. If they weren't going to answer him, he was damn sure going to find the answer somewhere.

"What are you, crazy?" Ten hands, much stronger than him held him down. The sheet was pulled tight against his chest until he thought he had been laced in a strait jacket.

Eric focused on one pair of eyes in particular. They were definitely a sight for his sore eyes.

"Settle down boy, before Mom cuts a switch."

"Nick." Emotion flooded him and he closed his eyes. He hadn't seen his brother since his wife's funeral over two years ago. His other brothers left the room giving them some privacy.

"Don't tell me you turned into a crybaby, Runt?" Nick teased, giving him a brief warm hug. His eyes were mysteriously damp, too.

"It's the medicine," Eric lied. "Are you back?"

"Yeah, for a while. I came back to bail my little brother out of a pail of hot water."

"What did I do besides defend Shayla? Have you met my daughter?" His words came out brokenly, he was so tired. But the love that enfolded his heart when he thought of Shayla was unsurpassed. He never thought he could feel this way about someone.

"Yeah I met her. She's a great kid. You sure picked two hellion cats to fall in love with."

"I know." Eric grabbed the sheet and pulled, loosening the cotton prison his brothers had him in. "I don't remember everything. Tell me what happened."

Nick laughed his eyes twinkling. "I heard this secondhand. But, it's rumored that the boy fainted when you went to punch him."

"But I remember hitting something."

"Oh, you hit something all right. Lauren is wearing your knuckle print squarely on her eye."

Eric let out a long string of curses.

Nick laughed again. "Don't tell me. Anyway, she verified that it was an accident. She was behind you trying to pull you off the kid and you reached back and socked her."

"You met Lauren?"

"Let's just say when we got here, the whole hospital knew who she was." Admiration tinged Nick's voice. "How you get these beautiful women, I'll never know. She was raging about the surgeon knowing where to put the knife. Something about not making any mistakes on the man she loved."

Eric's eyes widened in disbelief. "She said that?"

"That's a direct quote."

"Where is she?"

"The hospital gave her something to calm her down and the boy's mom was about to take her home. The last I saw her, she and Shayla were closeted together in a private waiting room, talking.'' Nick waited, then added, "She's a good kid, Eric. You're a very lucky man." His eyes grew wistful, then cleared. "Hold on, I'll get her." He walked to the door.

"Nick?"

He turned back and faced him. "Yeah, man?"

"I know the plane crash wasn't your fault. I don't blame you." His brother came back into view. This time his eyes glistened.

"Thanks." Nick said quietly. "I'm glad to hear you say that."

"Will you be here when I get out?"

"I'm back for a while. I'll send Shayla in."

Joy rose in him at his brother's answer. Eric closed his tired eyes. Lauren loved him. Shayla was at his side and Nick was home.

Life was damned good.

Chapter Twenty-Five

Lauren embraced Shayla for the first time in months. Almost more than she dreamed of she and Eric being together, she dreamed of reconciling with her daughter.

"I'm sorry," Shayla whispered, tears streaming from her eyes. The girl's sobs quieted some, yet Lauren still kept holding her.

Shayla's apology made her heart soar. Her sojourn into adulthood wasn't going to be easy. Lauren knew that and gently released her from the tight embrace.

"Hey, come on. We're both adults, we can talk about this." Her words hung between the two and Shayla finally met her gaze.

"Mom, I'm sorry. I'm so glad you said that. I want to be treated like an adult, but I realize I wasn't acting like one. I-I wanted you to respect me. I went off with Malik because I thought it would make me feel better inside that everybody was falling in love but me. I just wanted to be close to someone."

Lauren nodded understanding. "I'm sorry, too."

"Why?"

"For upsetting you. For falling in love with your father."

Shayla shook her head no. "I didn't mean for all of this to happen. I didn't mean for Daddy to punch you in the eye." Lauren grimaced remembering her swollen eye. "And I didn't mean for Daddy to get sick," she sniffled, her voice breaking. "I love you. I'm glad we're back together." She looked shyly at her mother. "Can you forgive me?"

It was time for Lauren to cry. "Of course," she said, while dabbing her leaking eyes. "I'll always love you. No matter what. But something has happened, uh, well—"

"You love Daddy," Shayla announced.

"Daddy?" she repeated, softly.

Shayla smiled again. "Yeah. I like calling him that." She looked at her hands and caressed the birthmark. "I love him and I love you. But I'm scared, too."

Lauren felt a tremendous weight lift off her heart. It was going to be all right. "Why?"

"Because, what if you two get together and then something happens? I won't have a family anymore. I'll have to choose and I don't want to do that. I want both of you."

She urged her daughter's head to rest on her shoulder.

"I love your father and he loves me. We're going to be together forever. You won't have to choose between us. We'll always be a family." Shayla's acceptance meant the world to her. She just couldn't imagine not being with Eric for the rest of her life.

The door opened and they both looked up. Lauren rose, her evening gown catching around her ankles. She stumbled toward the tall figure in the doorway. "Has something happened to Eric? Do I need to have a talk with the administrator?" she asked, stifling a yawn. Her voice sounded funny in her ears, too. Must be the shot they gave her earlier starting to take effect.

Nick grinned. "No, he's fine. In fact he'd like to see Shayla for a few minutes."

Shayla rushed past her out the door and disappeared down the hall.

"Come in," she said sleepily and staggered back to the couch. "If you just give me a minute, I'll ... I'll ..."

Nick gently covered Lauren with her coat, then motioned Rissa into the room. They introduced themselves as they stood inside the door staring at the sleeping figure on the couch.

"Looks like sleeping beauty and the prince have had quite a night."

"Yeah, it's been quite a night."

The door opened and Shayla came into view, her eyes red-rimmed and swollen. Eric lifted his arms to her and wrapped her in a loving embrace.

"Daddy, this is all my fault," she wailed, laying her head between his jaw and neck, sobbing.

He patted her back trying to soothe her. "I should have talked to you more about your relationship with Malik. Not just assumed that you were going to listen to me and do what I said." He stared at the birthmark that had brought them together. "I'm new at this—" Shayla cut him off.

"Tonight wasn't about Malik and me." She kneeled in the chair beside his bed and took his hand, tears dripping off her nose. Eric rested his head into the pillow and looked questioningly into her tear-rimmed eyes.

"What was it about then?"

"It's about you and Ma." She squeezed his hand and looked at him. Her eyes reflected insecurity and fear. "I didn't want you to love her more than you love me. You're my daddy." She sniffed loudly and wiped her nose on her sleeve. "I dreamed about how it would be if I ever found you. I promised myself that I would love no other person more than you."

Her words tore into his heart. Shayla had committed herself to loving him before she knew him. Years of dreaming of her life with her father were now true, and she wanted him to herself. She had said those exact words before. He wondered why he hadn't listened.

Lauren had been right all along. She knew of Shayla's insecurities and fears and somehow knew her daughter well enough to know that she would have a serious problem with their getting together.

"Shayla, I—"

"Wait. There's more." Her eyes glistened and chin trembled. "I love my mom. I miss her so much and I can't bear the thought of not seeing her every day. I know she loves you and you love her, maybe you can work something out, but—"

"But what?" Eric's heart raced hoping against hope that Shayla would see their love and feel it in her heart. He wasn't disappointed.

"When I thought I was going to lose you tonight"—her voice dropped to a whisper—"I thought of myself living alone with no one to love me. My mother loved me before I even came to live with her. And now you." She smiled, looking at him. "I'm almost a grown-up, and I don't want to be responsible for my mother or father missing out on their true love."

"When did you grow up?" he asked, his voice choked with emotion.

"Oh, sometime between Monday and today." She leaned her head on his hand and cried. Being an adult was exhausting. Eric stroked her head until her tears slowed.

"Have you talked to your mother?"

"Just now. We talked about a lot of things." She looked at his IV and dabbed fresh tears from her eyes. "She apologized for falling in love with you."

The medicine was taking effect and Lauren swam into his hallucination. Eric grasped his daughter's hand and held on.

"What did you say about that?" Her answer meant everything to him and he fought consciousness yearning to hear it.

"I said she had nothing to be sorry about. I love you both." He closed his eyes and drifted into the warm abyss of sleep. When he opened them again, Shayla was still at his side. "Daddy, are you awake?"

"Yeah, baby, I'm awake."

"I just wanted to tell you one more thing before I give Grandma a chance to come in." She leaned forward and stared into his eyes. "Malik and I didn't do anything. We decided to wait. Okay, Daddy?"

He was overjoyed at his promotion. That was what he wanted to hear all along. "Say it again."

"Huh?"

"Say it again." He croaked, his throat sore.

"We—"

Eric shook his head. "The last part." He struggled with the warm feeling seeping over him grasping at the residuals of consciousness.

"Daddy," she said softly. Then chanted, "Daddy, Daddy, Daddy . . ."

"Hello." Eric lifted the receiver of the phone in his home office and relished the break from the paperwork that crowded every space on the desk. Two weeks at home was enough to kill the healthiest man. But the one-year leave of absence from his practice to run the center was a dream come true.

"Hi, Eric. It's me, Lauren." He drew in a sharp breath and held it. Her voice flowed over him like an unexpected summer rain. Warm, wet, good.

"Hi."

"How are you feeling?"

"Fine."

"Oh. Good."

"The chicken soup was delicious," he said, then grimaced slapping his head. *The chicken soup was delicious? How about, I miss you, I love you, I want you with me? I'm sorry for giving you a black eye?*

"Thanks."

Silence fell again.

"How's your eye?"

She gave what he perceived as a laugh. "All better."

"Good." He couldn't speak past the lump in his throat. "I want to see you." *Better.*

"Eric, I was thinking that maybe I would bring it up to Shayla about moving back with home with me. Just until school is finished. Uh, I don't want to take her away from you while you're getting better . . ."

"I'm better," he said harshly. Silence ensued. Eric stared over the receiver of the phone at the sleeping figure of his daughter. She hadn't left his side since he came home eight days ago. She waited on him hand and foot and they talked. And talked and talked.

Everything was clear now, yet he and Lauren hadn't followed a good example. They hadn't talked about anything. That was going to change. "Lauren, I have a problem with that, to tell you the truth. Can we discuss this first?"

A defensive edge tainted her voice when she answered. "Sure. How about tonight after my set. Can you come by the club?"

"Yeah," he replied. "I'll be there."

Chapter Twenty-Six

Lauren peered out the stage door and felt a wave of panic sweep her again. There were so many people out tonight. Clutching her stomach trying to calm the nervous flutters, she admired the handsome black men and elegantly dressed black women who had chosen to spend the evening with her.

Her gaze swung back to the lone empty seat in front of the stage and she wanted so bad for Eric to be there. *He has to come before I lose my nerve.*

"About ready? The house is packed!" Jimmy's booming voice made her turn from her vigil at the door.

"Give me five more minutes, okay, Jimmy?" Lauren smiled at her longtime friend, so thankful to him. Even after she signed the record contract tomorrow, she wouldn't forget the man who gave her a chance when no one else would.

Grateful, she hugged him.

"Sorry honey, but I can't." He steered her from the door. "We're already half an hour late as it is."

He patted her shoulder as they walked toward the stage door.

"If he's worth anything, he'll show up." Jimmy B looked up from the desperate plea in her eyes and signaled the band to go on stage.

"Break a leg, honey." Left alone, Lauren steeled herself from the overwhelming disappointment. She hadn't expected Eric to stand her up. He said he would be there, so where was he?

The chords played for her entrance and she bounced on her toes and shrugged her shoulders, readying herself. Sing for them, she thought as she walked on stage to thunderous applause. Sing for the one hundred and fifty people who paid fifty dollars a ticket, to spend an evening with me.

Lauren was pouring her heart and soul into the number and Eric hurried from the car lot to the line outside the door. *Move it*. He demanded inwardly wishing the people in line would get the hell out of his way. He *had* to get inside.

Still a little stiff from the surgery, he knew he shouldn't be outside, but he gave Lauren his word he would be there. He wasn't about to let a line stop him from seeing her. He stepped out of line and walked quickly around the building. The back entrance was shadowed and poorly lit, but he was determined. He questioned his judgment once in the alley's darkness. How many mugging victims had he stitched as a resident at Grady Hospital for not using common sense?

The rustling sounds from deep within the alley were like the warning siren on a tug boat and he stopped halfway between the door and the noise.

"I've been waiting for you," the coarse voice said.

Eric braced himself for the attack he felt was imminent, focusing on the direction the voice had come from. He estimated the distance out of the alley and cringed. If the guy had a weapon, he wouldn't stand a chance making it out without more injury. I'll have to take my chances.

Talking or fighting.

"What do you want, money? Take it." He dug for his wallet. "I just want to walk through that door," Eric prayed as the looming figure approached. The faded glow from the street light proved useless in identifying the menace behind the cool voice.

"No, I mean I really have been waiting for you." He stepped from the shadows.

"PeeWee!" Eric exhaled sharply. "Man, you scared the crap out of me." Relief flooded him as the linebacker-sized man opened the back door. "Why are you waiting for me?"

"Lauren asked me to keep an eye out for you."

"I'm glad to see it's you." Eric followed him inside. "I'll talk to her after the show. There probably aren't any seats left," he said, relieved to be out of the alley. Relieved he wasn't about to die. PeeWee slapped a meaty hand on his back and propelled him down the hallway at top speed.

"You're just in time for the last number. Go through this door, and around the front of the stage. There's one empty seat left."

"Thanks, man," Eric said, the space between his shoulders blades stinging. It was forgotten quickly, the anticipation of seeing Lauren overshadowing any pain.

Her bare back was to him as he entered the candlelit room and she belted out the final notes of the song.

Eric claimed the empty seat, and felt his heart begin a quick staccato beat when she glided as if on a cloud, center stage, and smiled at him.

The usual easy sway of her hips was more pronounced beneath the clinging white dress she wore. Eric kept his eyes fixed on the seductive pendulum motion, until he felt his body scream for air and he breathed, dragging his eyes higher only to become entranced with the provocative slope of her vanilla covered breasts.

Lauren smiled seductively saying, "Thank you," to the audience. "I wrote this song," she waved away the stool the stage hand positioned behind her. "Thanks, Bryant, I won't need that."

The crowd cheered when he bowed, blowing her a kiss.

"So"—her attention was drawn back to the audience. Eric met her gaze fully—"let me know if you like it." She positioned the microphone on the stand. Then Lauren raised her hands in the air, arched her back, and bringing them around, slid her hands over her hips to her buttocks, ending on her thighs. The crowd went wild and she sang.

"Once upon a time, I believed in fairy tales, of sugar plums and hopping bunnies, of dark knights and beautiful castles," her eyes sparkled and she paused, inhaling before she continued.

"But now I'm all grown up, and I know what love is all about."

"Its moved my feet, taken me to hell and back, its hurt so bad I thought I would die from its hard cold slap.

"But late into the night, as I lay alone, I would look out and see the stars and know somewhere out there was a sweet love."

She raised the microphone from the stand, lifted her dress out of the way, and walked down the front steps of the stage. And stood before him. The woman he would grow old with, the mother of his children, his soul-mate sang her heart out to him in a love song. Her hazel eyes glowed like golden fire as she continued.

"Oooh, baby, you came into my life when I was sure there was no hope of love for me.

"I searched high and low for someone to care for me. But just when I'd given up, decided loneliness would be my mate forever..."

The music reached a rich crescendo. She reached out her hand and caressed his cheek, then tilted his chin up.

"You walked into my life and branded me your queen. Spoiled me and caressed me, showing me what real love could truly mean."

Eric raised his hand and there was a collective gasp from the audience when she placed it over her heart, sliding her hand beneath his.

"And even when I walked away, you followed, taking my hand, bringing me back into your silken cocoon.

"You jump started my heart"—neither heard the thunderous response when their joined hands imitated the pulse of a beating heart—*"and made me love you, I can't stand to be alone, I want to grow old with you, Baby, please, please, let me love you."* Lauren smiled through her tears and eased down. He folded her onto his lap and held on.

"My heart won't lie, that's why I can't deny." She paused, touching her finger to her lips, quieting the uproarious crowd. *"What we have is a sweet silken love."*

Lauren carried the final note, letting it fade slowly away. The last chords of the music played and she was still, the microphone in her hands, lowering to her lap.

She opened her eyes and met his gaze.

Everything around them disappeared like morning dew in sunshine. The standing ovation from the applauding crowd, even the smiles from her friends at their table. She wound her arms around his neck, her breasts pressing into his chest.

Their tongues met first, outside their mouths until his lips covered hers. Every sane thought was snatched away as her taste and texture filled the blank spaces.

He dipped her back, his heart soaring.

She had written that song for them.

He couldn't help how much he loved her at that moment. It was eons before he pulled his lips from hers. A deafening noise like thunder broke into his passion, and he realized it was the crowd applauding them. Eric drew his mouth back from Lauren's, but kept his hands firmly around her waist. He wasn't ever going to let her go. She raised the microphone to her lips.

"I'm in love with you."

Chapter Twenty-Seven

Eric lowered Lauren's bare feet to the floor of her candle-filled bedroom for just a second. In that short span of time, he threw off his jacket and began to unbutton his shirt. When she tried to walk away, he captured her to him again claiming her mouth unable to control the fiery hunger that threatened to over run its banks.

"Eric," she called breathlessly.

"Mmm?"

"The candles." She groaned when his teeth sought her pleasure points on the back of her neck.

"Later," he whispered, lifting her in his arms carrying her to the bed.

He placed her in the center and sat behind her. He kissed her shoulder, his tongue leaving a cool wet path. She bowed her back into his chest shuddering as he touched lower and lower.

Lauren sucked her breath between her teeth, and he growled, the carnal noises making flames of desire leap into his eyes. He didn't claim them with his mouth right away as she hoped when she arched her back to him.

No, Eric closed his eyes and memorized their beauty through his hands. He stroked them into shape until they pointed like the tips of a chocolate covered glacier. Just when her feet slapped the bed in abandon, he claimed the first with his mouth, his hand still working the other.

Lauren screamed. She couldn't help herself.

"Why are you torturing me?" she moaned, her body uncontrollable as she thrashed against the bed.

"Because I want to take you with me to see the stars."

Lauren lost track of time as he undressed himself then her and joined her on the bed. All she knew was that seeing him naked was better than seeing anything else in the world.

His bronze skin was slick with a thin sheen of moisture and when he gathered her in his arms, his erection throbbing between them, she moved her hips wanting to end her own suffering. Lightly she touched his scar. "Does it hurt?"

"No." He turned her on her stomach. "This hurts." He covered her body with his. His erection pressed against her behind, and she curled up.

His hands so capable and gentle, lifted her, plunging through thick hair, seeking her womanhood. He parted her with his hands, teasing her with the tip of his erection.

"Yes, Eric, please," she moaned into the blankets. Lauren lifted her head wanting to turn over and end the sensual madness, but she couldn't. He claimed her mouth in a hot wet kiss, his hand stroking from her neck and over her breasts.

"Lay down, sweetie," he said. "We're not done."

"Ooo . . ." She fell face down on the bed, moaning.

Eric scratched her back with his beard, covering the burning in its wake with wet kisses. Then she found out the true purpose of the backs of her knees and the insides of her ankles. She lay back down and turned knowing her climax was approaching, especially if he did what she thought he would do.

"Oh, please," she begged, then buried her face in the pillows.

His large hand spanned her waist and she flipped over reaching her hands out to touch him.

"If you do that, I won't be able to hold on and wait for you." He smiled like Felix the cat, and bent down claiming her with his mouth. He replaced his tongue with his thumb, stroking her until she burst into rockets of gasps and screams and tears and moans.

Then he entered her. Lauren's final contractions gripped him and Eric knew for sure, this was the best pleasure known to man.

Pity the man who had never felt this good.

He plunged deep into her quickening the pace when her legs wrapped around his waist and she urged him with her mouth against his erect nipples.

Eric grabbed the bed above her head and deepened his thrust oblivious to the sweat that trickled down his face and dropped on her nose from his.

"Lauren," he called her name again and again approaching the edge faster. Curling to be closer to her, he planted his mouth against hers, his "Ahhh" making her smile. Finally, his toes flexed, the backs of his legs tensed, and he pushed hard one last time, strong and long as he released all his seed into her.

The room hadn't righted itself on its spinning axis so Lauren closed her eyes and lay her head against Eric's broad chest.

He hadn't just come. No, he said something when he came she was sure he didn't know had tumbled from his lips.

His words bounced in her head and she felt light and airy from them.

"Marry me." It was too much to think he could want her to be his wife. Eric shifted her on top of him and stroked her back with the ease of a man who had what he wanted. But would he want her and all her new responsibilities.

"You didn't answer me." His gray eyes bored into hers. "Hey, what's the matter?"

"Nothing." She fought to control the quiver in her voice. "I have something to tell you." Holding his hands, she wrapped them around her stomach and looked lovingly at him.

"I—"

"What? Go ahead." His index finger strolled down each vertebrae on her back, then up again.

"I don't know if you'll want to marry me. I don't know anything anymore." She eased away from him and gathered the covers around her. "Last week, I was offered a record deal. It's Blackbelt records out of New York. They want me." She couldn't disguise her excitement.

"My dream has finally come true," her voice dropped. "I don't know if I can let it go."

"When do you have to be there?" Eric crossed the room to the window and stood with his back to her. This was exactly what she feared. That he wouldn't want her to do it. She hated to choose and really there was no choice. She wanted him and Shayla. But this . . . this was her dream come true.

"Eric," the sob tore from her lips. "Don't make me choose."

"I won't. There is no choice. You have to go."

Shocked, she held her hands over her heart. "What did you say?"

"You have to go." Turning from the window, he stood bare and proud and a bright smile on his face. His arrowed erection honed in on her desire. She laid back accepting his weight on her. "And I'm going with you." He pressed into her warm wetness. "We're going to see your dreams come true together. No more of us being alone." He touched his lips to hers meeting her love-filled gaze. "Our daughter has two parents. She's going to live with two parents."

Lauren's fingers raked his back and he gentled his stroke. "I love you, Lauren. Say you'll marry me."

"I'll do better than that," she said in a husky, sexy voice. Lauren embraced his body with hers. "Yes, yes, yes."

It was what he waited all his life to hear.

Dear Reader:

My dream has come true! I've always dreamed of being an entertainer. Moving crowds of people with my voice or actions played in my mind from the time I was a small child. I can't sing nor act, but I've learned that I am a storyteller. Amazed best describes how I feel. Blessed bespeaks what I am.

I appreciate all the wonderful fan mail and comments about *Now or Never* and *Whisper To Me* in *Silver Bells*. I look forward to hearing from you regarding *Silken Love* and am excited to announce *Keeping Secrets* will be in stores March 1998.

I appreciate all of you and ask that you keep me in your prayers. Correspondence is welcome. Please enclose a SASE. My address is P.O. Box 956455. Duluth, Georgia, 30095-9508.

Enjoy,

Carmen

ABOUT THE AUTHOR

Carmen Green was born in Buffalo, New York. She received a bachelor of arts degree in English from Fredonia State University College in Fredonia, New York.

She currently resides in Georgia with her husband and children.